MW01134297

# Ava Again

## *A sequel to "Ava"*

JANET PERRONI

# AVA AGAIN
## A SEQUEL TO "AVA"

iUniverse books may be ordered through booksellers or by contacting:

iUniverse
1663 Liberty Drive
Bloomington, IN 47403
www.iuniverse.com
844-349-9409

ISBN: 978-1-6632-4892-3 (sc)
ISBN: 978-1-6632-4893-0 (e)

Library of Congress Control Number: 2022922891

Print information available on the last page.

iUniverse rev. date:  12/20/2022

In the pageantry of life, we display numerous facades, but with integrity and righteousness as our guides, true happiness will be our legacy.

To my family: Jerry, Lauren, Scott, Tony, Joseph, and Peter—with love!

# PROLOGUE

Ava stood in the kitchen of her small, sparsely furnished, rented flat in Boston, Massachusetts. She looked at her only son, Trevor. At fifteen years old, he was the image of his father—at least what she could remember of him. She reminisced about how she had gone to Falcon Seaport to find Alistar—that was sixteen years ago, not long after the Great War had ended—but his naval ship had already left, and with it, her heart. She vividly recalled her feelings of loneliness and despair; she'd been left pregnant and unaware of the struggles she would endure. The tears she had shed had felt like a river flowing down her face, while inside terror had raged like hot lava. The anxiety and fear of the unknown later would erupt like a volcano.

Little did she know of the nightmarish labyrinth she would have to navigate alone. First, her father had beaten her for being pregnant. Then her uncle had attempted a sexual assault. Later as her baby belly expanded to the point that she no longer could conceal it, people looked at her with disdain. Society disparaged anyone who didn't fit the social norms. Countless obscenities were hurled at her, along with lingering whispers behind her back. When

Trevor was born she had lived with the stigma of being an unwed mother, which meant she was viewed as sexually easy. She had to move out of the family home and get her own apartment because of her scandalous reputation. It had been rough for her and difficult to find a place to live. In the city, there were beggars in dirty, malodorous clothing on every corner. Lack of proper hygiene and food meant diseases were prevalent, although the world, thankfully, was beginning to recover from the influenza pandemic.

When Ava couldn't pay the rent, she had to barter sex acts with her perverted landlord; he had used her body and had taken what he wanted, physically and mentally. Disgusting forced intercourse befouled her to the point where she could no longer take it. Eventually she made reparation with her family who encouraged her to return home.

Shortly thereafter, she was hired as domestic help for a wealthy family in Brookline, where she soon fell madly in love with their handsome builder son, Devon. After a magical affair with him that took them to romantic Italy, she was astounded to find herself pregnant for the second time. Devon's estranged wife, Jane, returned; she was a mastermind of deception and manipulated him with her female allure into coitus. Jane had become pregnant by an old boyfriend but deceived Devon into thinking he was the father. Ava was shocked when she overheard their lovemaking and disgusted when, as their maid, she was required to clean their bed sheets. She knew that Devon was not the father of Jane's baby, as she and Devon had been in Italy together at the time of conception. Later, Devon informed Ava that he was reuniting with Jane, as she had threatened to ruin his business with a messy divorce, which would destroy him, and to take away their son.

Soon, Jane and Ava had a confrontation, as Jane had found out about Ava's affair with Devon. Consequently, Ava's employment was terminated, and she succumbed to psychiatric depression, even as her uterus expanded with the fetus inside her. She even attempted suicide by sticking her head in a gas oven. Vivid memories of that desperate act haunted her inner core. She would always carry the image of the gas flames almost scorching her porcelain skin as she passed out. When she awoke, she found herself in the hospital; she had already delivered the baby. The nurses named the baby Mary, after the Virgin Mother. Mary wasn't expected to live but she did.

Later, Ava's father arranged for her to marry a man from England named Scott, who was in desperate need of immigration paperwork to stay in America; he needed an American wife. Unfortunately, he was already married.

Devon eventually discovered Jane's deception, and he left her, but Ava was already married to Scott and had five more children by him. It was too late for Ava and Devon to reunite. The Great Depression gripped the country, and Devon became an alcoholic to cope with his material loss—and the loss of Ava.

Ava suspected Scott was a bigamist. She believed he had deserted a wife and a couple of children. Somehow, she managed not to let his abandonment history plague her thoughts, even though she knew damn well he could do it to her. Fortunately, Ava and Scott did well together, although money was scarce, and there were bread lines to help people survive. Most people were poor; when the stock market had collapsed, desperate people had committed suicide by jumping out of tall buildings when they lost all their money.

Scott earned a meager salary as a baker, but they did have food when he was employed. Food was very limited, and fried cabbage with seasoning was a main staple. He would take home food remnants like stale bread and make something out of nothing. He would take bacon fat and make it into a flavorful gravy and serve it for dinner. The children would dip the hard bread into the gravy to soften it. It was quite delicious, and the children said it was one of their favorite meals.

Unexpectedly, Scott had a massive stroke, forcing him to live within the physical and mental limitations of his condition. Everyone in the family had to adjust to his being confined to a wheelchair. It was difficult for Ava to care for Scott in addition to all the children; sometimes, it seemed impossible. Yet she persevered and carried out the daily activities of raising the children and running the household. Her strong will and inner strength created her motivation.

# CHAPTER ONE

# Reality

Ava, now in her mid-thirties, had only a few wrinkles on her pretty Irish face. A few strands of silver-gray ran through her thick dark-brown hair, which she usually wore in a ponytail. She carried a few extra pounds on her petite frame, so she was very curvy with large breasts, which always seemed to be the first thing someone noticed about her.

Thick steam came from the three pots on the stove as Ava stirred each one vigorously.

"I'm hungry," Trevor announced to his mother as he walked into the disorderly kitchen. He did this at least five times each day. He squinted his blue eyes and rolled up his lower lip in an exaggerated face. Pubescent facial hair was starting to appear on his face as a shadow. His pencil-straight dark-blond hair, which needed to be cut, fell over his forehead as he frowned.

"No snacking between meals," Ava told him. "You know we don't have much food. We barely have enough

1

for you and all your siblings. Now that Dad is sick makes it even worse …" she sighed. "Drink some water until suppertime."

Trevor reached for the chipped water pitcher on the table and filled his glass. He gulped down the water in a matter of seconds. Then he repeated the process.

"I know it's tough to be hungry, especially since you're growing into manhood," Ava said gently. "The Lord will consider all our hardships on earth. He only gives us what he knows we can tolerate." Ava was a devout Catholic; she hoped her words to her son made sense. She felt awful that he was hungry, but they didn't have enough food to go around.

She was making "Hoover Stew" that day, named after former President Herbert Hoover, who had been blamed for mismanagement of American farms. He had required mass production of products to help Europe after the Great War but never gave the farmers the financial backing or equipment to harvest and distribute the food. He had required all cows to be tested for tuberculosis too. Everything became more complicated with the locust invasions and the Dust Bowl. The stew Ava was making took its name from Hoover because he was blamed for the unbearable economic conditions. It consisted primarily of macaroni, hot dogs, tomatoes, and corn—when such food was available.

It was easily understandable that Franklin D. Roosevelt had won the presidential race. He was trying to reverse and repair unemployment, as well as the banking crisis, with his New Deal. It would take time to see if it would work to improve the food chain and Americans' lifestyles.

Mary, who was fourteen, came into the kitchen, and Ava instructed her to add more water to the soup that was in another pot on the stove and to cut the carrots. This was exactly what Ava had done when she was young, as she had been the caretaker for her younger sister, Kaelyn. It was a picture of historical duplication. For Ava, the picture now consisted of seven children—five with Scott, as well as her first two children, fathered by Alistar and Devon, respectively. Because Scott needed extensive comprehensive care, the situation was even more difficult.

Mary was like a second mother to the rest of the children, whose ages ranged from two to ten. Her responsibility was to wash their faces daily, change the diapers of the youngest, and dress the older ones for school. She also made sure they were bathed weekly. At times, it seemed like a factory assembly line of hygiene. In a sense, Mary fulfilled the role that Ava had performed for her family while growing up as main caretaker for her younger sister, Kaelyn.

Kaelyn had married well and had three children. She had a good life and didn't have to work or deal with any hardships. Ava envied her sister, as she had practically raised her. Sometimes Kaelyn would offer to care for Ava's children, but it wasn't very often. Ava's mother also would offer to assist but she was old and frail now; she couldn't quite manage all the kids.

Evan, Ava's father, didn't come around much. He was retired and found comfort in the local bars. Prohibition had ended, so her father had numerous places to go and socialize now. The family would have large Irish gatherings at Ava's parents' house for the Catholic holidays. Kaelyn's children would be poised and sit still on the couch. Ava's brood would run around, causing a lot of commotion. The difference between them was like night and day. The bottom line was that Ava had so many kids that it was impossible to control them. Since Scott's stroke and subsequent limited mobility, however, Ava and the kids couldn't go to holiday festivities at her parents' house.

Trevor would help Ava with Scott, getting him out of the wheelchair and caring for him, which was a physical challenge. Scott's atrophied muscles seemed to shrink, resulting in extreme contractures. His mental state deteriorated, and he would suffer from hallucinations. When this occurred, he would scream nonsense phrases. The younger children would become upset by his screaming, and they, in turn, would start yelling. There was an echoing tunnel of noise that reverberated and vibrated into the walls of the tiny apartment. The walls seemed to soak up the noise and bounce it back into the room. Scott lived alone in his own world of physical and mental torment.

Ava had appealed to the local church for assistance, and they frequently sent her food and a little money. She was behind in the rent and knew they soon would have to move. Ava had no clue what she should do. Her brother, Jerry, who had never married, would give her a little money at times. The two of them had become close throughout the years, and she valued everything he did for her and the children. He was a true guardian angel for the family.

Trevor physically cared for Scott as much as possible, and Ava was in awe when she saw his compassion with his stepfather. This man was not Trevor's biological father, but Trevor accepted the responsibility of caring for him in a loving manner, no questions asked. It almost seemed unfair to Ava that Trevor had this burden placed upon him.

One day, Trevor went into the living room to check on Scott, but this time there was something different. Scott was in a slightly more contorted position, and he had a blank stare. He was not moving at all, his eyes did not blink, and his skin was cold.

Trevor frantically yelled to his mother, "Come quickly!"

Ava ran from the kitchen and shook her husband. "Scott! Scott! Scott!" she screamed. "Trevor, get the doctor!" She stood there, stunned, and all she could do was cry. She didn't want to admit it, but she knew that he had passed. Then she realized that her other six children had come into the room because of the commotion. As they gathered around Scott, Ava had a tough time controlling her emotions; she felt emotionally ambushed and was mentally and physically shocked. This couldn't be happening! Scott was father to all the children!

Each child kept randomly repeating, "Why isn't he moving, Mommy?" Their words echoed in Ava's head, and she knew she had to take control of the situation quickly. She instructed Mary to take the children to their bedrooms. When they were out of the room, she felt Scott's chest to see if she could detect a heartbeat. She felt only the coldness and stiffness of his skin beneath her palms. She did not see or feel any respiration coming from him either. In her mind, she said a prayer for him. There was stillness in the air; his soul had left his body, and all that remained was an abundance of cold calmness, as time seemed to stop. Hot tears flowed from her eyes, as if a rain cloud had burst open. She physically shook with emotion and sobbed uncontrollably.

Scott's wake was in the small living room of their flat. Although it was the custom, it was very emotional for Ava to have the wake there, knowing that Scott was still present but not alive. Most of the children didn't understand the situation—they wanted to see Daddy— and the small flat seemed to exude gloom.

Ava placed a small table at the head of his pine casket, on which she set a small photograph she had found of Scott, taken somewhere in England. In it, he was wearing his knickerbocker pants and spats while standing with his parents. Beside that photograph she placed their wedding photo. Those were the only two photographs she had of him. She wasn't sure if she should notify his family in England, but she had no idea how to get in touch with them anyway. Scott had never spoken of his family, and Ava believed that was so he could keep the secret of his first marriage in England to himself. Still, she only suspected that he'd still been married; she never had any proof.

Ava was practically oblivious to the condolences she received from the visitors who came to pay their respects. There was repeated handshaking and hugging, but she felt little of it as she stood, emotionless, like a statue. She did feel the pronounced pain of her swollen eyes from all the crying she had done over the past few days. There were severe red marks on her skin where she had wiped the tears from her face.

Ava wore a thick, black-lace veil to shield her—it concealed the constant flow of tears. Her head was numb from the tension and crying. The children also cried constantly, although Ava thought that most of them were in denial, even as they saw Scott's distorted, lifeless body in the pine casket. His stiff body still looked somewhat contorted from the effects of the stroke. She knew that when he had the stroke that dark sorrow would approach at some point to close the book of his life. No matter how Ava tried to prepare for his death, though, it had reached out and grabbed him and her unexpectedly. This was the first time the children had to deal with a death in the family, especially difficult because he was so close to them. In Ava's mind, however, he had been dead to living since his stroke.

Kaelyn and her family came, and she tried to be as supportive as she could. Kaelyn was caring for their parents at that point, as they were getting very old. All of Ava's brothers came too, except Mitt, who was the family drunk. He lived in a bizarre cycle of soberness and then a drunken haze on the streets. He was always a family embarrassment and never did much except drink.

Ava's parents and family were supportive of her, but it was almost unbearable for her. Then, after three days, it was over. Ava came to the grim reality that she was totally alone—with seven children. She thought of the times before when she was totally alone—before she'd had two babies, Trevor and Mary, and before Scott had married her.

Just four years earlier, Devon, the man she truly loved, was hit by a car and killed. He had become an alcoholic and had lost almost everything. The Great Depression was difficult for everyone. Ava thought of the time she went to his funeral. She hid inconspicuously behind a tree and wept for him. Although they were never together again, he was always in her heart. She had used the expensive pearl necklace he had given her as a set of rosary beads to pray for him. Devon was engraved on her heart, and she knew they were soul mates. She was glad they had experienced total love, even though he was gone from this earth. He had come into her life and had remained perpetually in her heart, despite death taking him too soon. She hoped that, somehow, they would be together again in another universe.

The demands of motherhood and surviving each day were very chaotic and challenging. Now she was totally alone. Scott had been a good father; he could break up the children's fighting and make them listen to him. Later, though, when he was immobile in the wheelchair, he couldn't assist Ava in any way. She had to adapt and reinvent herself to keep her household going. That wasn't so different now; she knew it was all up to her, and all the children relied on her. They were living in a different dimension now, and *survival* took on new meaning for her.

The next night, just as the children had fallen asleep and the apartment became quiet, the front door buzzer sounded. Someone kept pressing it, so Ava answered it, only to find a stout, balding, middle-aged man in a suit.

"Are you Ava Daly?" he asked without preamble.

"Yes, um, I was until I married Scott Callott. Daly was my maiden name."

"Did you know Devon McDougal? Did you have a baby by him?" he asked abruptly.

She stared at the man without answering. She couldn't believe what she was hearing! She wanted to leave her past in the past. She had spent decades trying to conceal Mary's and Trevor's birth records because they had different fathers. She thought how horrifying it was to have people scorn her for being unwed and pregnant— and it had happened twice! It wasn't until Scott came along and married her that she finally had some sort of respectability.

When she didn't respond, the man took a step back and said slowly, "I am Leon Woods, the attorney for the late Lady Tatum, Devon McDougal's mother. She died recently, and we are reading her will tomorrow at her estate. You should be there."

"Devon's mother? What would I have to do with her will?" Ava asked, clearly mystified.

"Your presence is requested, per the will. I can't say

any more until the will is read publicly, which is tomorrow. Sorry that I couldn't have given you more notice, but frankly, I couldn't find you."

Ava was shocked and remained silent. Devon, the man she truly had loved and who was Mary's father, had died years earlier—and now they wanted her? Why? Old memories resurfaced in her mind, especially of the time when she was dismissed from her job as the maid. That was when she was pregnant with Mary.

"Please tell me that you will come," he said.

"I … will try," she stammered.

Mr. Woods wrote down the address on a piece of paper, handed it to her, and briskly left.

As she stood at the door, Ava reflected on her past. She wasn't sure if she was motivated by fate or by herself, but she knew that sexual desire for Devon had taken her down an unwise road.

The following day, she dressed in the same suit she had worn for Scott's funeral. She rode the trolley to Brookline, as she had done when she was employed by the family. Everything seemed like such a flashback to another time. Before long, she reached the trolley platform, where she walked down the hill and onto the sidewalk that led to the estate. It stood grander than ever, towering over the shrubbery in front of the estate and set back against the trees, with the picturesque farm in the background. She could see the stables where she and Devon had their first sexual encounter. She remembered how magnificent it was and he was—in so many ways.

A flood of emotion enveloped her as she thought back to her time with Devon. She had truly loved him so much. She felt as if she had entered a parallel universe, where she saw a lustrous yet transparent vision of Devon and her engaging in sex. He had steely shoulders and an impeccable, muscular physique. Slight graying at his temples seemed to frame his handsome face in a regal manner. She saw a ghostlike image of him placing a plaid blanket over a small hay bale in the barn and then gently placing her on top of the blanket. Then, in almost one sweep, he lifted her skirt, pulled her panties down, undid his fly, and inserted himself within the prison of her tactile desires and physical needs of her vaginal canal. She remembered her temperature rising and her skin turning crimson in a colossal explosion as they joined together. Excited neurons and synapses resulted in an explosion of human nature between them. Oh, what a delicious and delirious climax it was! How good they were together.

Reluctantly, she shook off her reverie and strolled up the winding brick path to the front door. Still, her head flooded with memories, as if Devon was smiling at her. There was a slight warm breeze that almost encased her, as if she was frozen in time, as she rang the doorbell on the front door. She was lost in a memory when Jane, Devon's ex-wife, opened the door to her.

Jane looked slightly aged; fine lines rippled around her eyes, but she still was beautiful with her smooth porcelain skin contrasted against her coal-black hair. Her silky hair was pinned back in a long braid that twisted around the crown of her head.

*That style is Jane's version of creating a tiara or halo over her head*, Ava thought. *She was always so conceited!*

"You! *You!*" Jane spat out. "You dirty tramp! What are you doing here? You stole my husband and had a bastard baby by him!" Jane's voice rose in volume with each word until she was screaming. "You have a nerve, coming here! You think that we owe you something? You slut shit!"

*Careful!* Ava warned herself. *What on earth was I thinking, coming here?* Here stood an obviously volatile woman, her archenemy and nemesis, condemning her by swirling insult after insult at her. Ava cringed at Jane's humiliating and offensive words.

Suddenly, behind Jane appeared Mr. Woods, the attorney who had come to Ava's home. He unobtrusively slid in between the two women and practically hovered in front of Jane. Physically this pushed Jane's body backward and blocked her comments breaking the negative magnetic field that was holding the two women. Maintaining as calm a demeanor as possible, he gestured with his forearm and politely invited Ava in.

Ava silently, almost mechanically, moved through the doorway. She knew there were advantages and disadvantages to being there. The closing of the front door seemed to symbolize the end to Ava's fantasy with Devon and their together one last time. Now, she was thrown into a corrosive situation that caused an immediate feeling of despair. She assumed she was there because of Mary: their love child. She would just have to deal with Jane and her humiliating, hostile, and nasty comments. *Jane deceived Devon*, Ava remembered. *She became pregnant by another man so who is she to talk about being a slut?*

Once inside the large foyer, which Ava used to clean, she refused to look in Jane's direction. Instead, she looked at her surroundings and could see that things in the house had changed. Now, it was meagerly decorated.

Mr. Woods motioned for everyone to enter the library and invited them to take a seat. As Ava entered, she saw Brendon, Devon's son. *He's all grown up*, she thought. *Of course, he would be.* She murmured her condolences to him when he glanced in her direction. He acknowledged her by raising his eyebrows and giving a silent nod.

Jane entered the library and sat beside Brendon.

Ava took a seat in the back row, across the room, which was as far as possible away from Jane and Brendon. She didn't recognize the people who sat next to her, but she assumed they were relatives. She decided she was in a safe zone, away from immediate-family contact. She presumed that everyone knew she'd had a baby with Devon. When she looked to her side, she realized she was sitting beside Kira.

Kira nodded to Ava as they recognized each other. Kira was the full-time maid that Ava had worked with when she was employed by the family.

When everyone was seated, Mr. Woods quickly introduced himself as the McDougal family attorney. "You all have been invited here today for the reading of the late Lady Tatum's will. We all knew her as a wonderful woman who was not only kind to all but also dedicated to our Brookline community. In her long life, she worked tirelessly to promote housing and food for people who had less than she had. Even though the Great Depression robbed most of us of our possessions and our self-esteem, somehow Lady Tatum struggled forward and continued to assist people less fortunate than herself. At one point, she used the estate here as a bed-and-breakfast, which helped her to survive. She did this in the sunset of her life, but she did manage to save her home from bankruptcy. Today, I have gathered everyone to formally read her will. The estate is to be sold and all her assets are to be pooled."

He then read directly from the will. "Seventy-five percent of the amount shall go to my grandson, Brendon. Brendon may or may not support his mother with his funds; that will be up to him. I made this provision because my former daughter-in-law and my son are divorced. To my devoted maid and caretaker, Kira, I leave $10,000, for all the years she remained faithful to me. I leave $5,000 to each cousin and relative. Lastly, I leave my other grandchild, Mary, $2,000, to be set up in a trust to purchase a home for her. Her mother, Ava, will oversee the money, but it must be used to purchase real estate and for Mary's care."

Everyone remained in solemn silence. Then Brendon stood up. He obviously was trying to organize his thoughts and skillfully tried to usher people out, grimly stating, "Thank you for coming...everyone."

Jane screamed, and her face twisted in anger. "That is not fair!" she yelled hysterically, her head shaking furiously back and forth. "No, no, no!"

Brendon put his hand on his mother's shoulder, attempting to calm her outburst.

"*She*—the lying, husband-stealing bitch—gets more than me! Oh no! I will contest the will!" Jane yelled in a deafening tone. She launched herself into a standing position, with her fists raised toward the back of the room in Ava's direction.

"Mom, calm down!" Brendon said.

In the strained atmosphere of the room, all the others sat silently as they watched Jane's outburst.

Ava glanced at Kira, who shrugged her shoulders ever so faintly but remained silent. Clearly, Kira was not going to be supportive or get involved in this verbal brawl. Ava found the courage and stood up. All eyes were on her now. She did not want to return to the past and Jane's scalding insults. She hesitated, then turned to walk out of the library. When she reached the library's double doors, she glanced back in the room and gave a strained smile, followed by a laugh under her breath as Jane was still carrying on.

Taking several deep breaths, she made it to the front door. It felt as if she was being infused with anxiety, and her nerves were totally rattled. She could feel herself shaking all over. She stiffly walked down the front pathway.

"Stop, stop!" Mr. Woods loudly yelled as he waved his arms in the air.

Ava stopped and turned to face him.

"I will be in touch with the details of Mary's inheritance," he told Ava.

Ava nodded and resumed walking. Kira caught up

to her, and together, they strolled slowly to the street in front of the house.

"It is good to see you," Kira said.

"Yes, it is good to see you too," Ava replied sincerely—but cautiously, as Kira had seen her and Devon in sexual interludes at least twice. Ava felt embarrassed but still lingered on the memory of how well Devon could satisfy her natural desires. Now, she had a glint in her eyes and felt triumphant that Lady Tatum had given her something. She needed it so much now to get by!

Kira snickered and said, "You got more than Jane! Lady Tatum was sure mad with Jane when she found out she tried to deceive Devon by passing off her daughter, Taylor, as Devon's baby. It was tough on her, as she was old and alone. Her husband died shortly after Devon's death. Then, after she sold almost everything, she started to rent rooms to survive. She would have to wash the sheets and put them through the wringer. It was difficult for her to do the stretching and pulling of the sheets through the machine as she had arthritis in her joints. I used to drop by and clean the house for her once in a while. One time, she had a massive infestation of bedbugs—what a nightmare that was! Brendon stayed around, but he was in college, and had to study so he wasn't much help. Did you see the farm area?"

"Yes, I glanced out the window when we were sitting there," Ava answered. Her memory of Devon and her resurfaced again. She could see their appetizing and scrumptious lovemaking in the barn. She didn't think that Kira knew about that time. Ava conjured in her mind the time when Kira caught her giving Devon oral sex at his desk. She was so embarrassed!

"Well, everything is overgrown now. Nature has taken over," Kira said. "They sold the cows and the horses. Sad how this depression robbed almost everyone."

"Yes, some people even jumped out the windows of the tall office buildings when the market crashed," added Ava.

Kira gave a determined nod. "You and I never really had anything to lose. We were always poor and just getting by. I always thought that Devon and you would end up together somehow, some way."

Ava hesitated a moment but then wholeheartedly responded, "He was and always will be in my heart."

"He died a drunk, you know? He was crossing Route 9 when he was hit by a car. Speculation has it that he was going from one bar to another."

Ava did not like Kira putting him down like he was a bum. When Kira and she worked together, there always seemed to be friction, as Kira did not approve of Ava's relationship with Devon. Kira clearly was jealous of them, and she would belittle Ava with her occasional malicious comments, accompanied by surly facial expressions.

Ava decided that her best approach right now was to withdraw from this conversation, so she quickly said, "I must go now. Nice to have seen you."

"Oh wait!" Kira said, putting her hand on Ava's arm. "Did you know that Brendon was the one who found Devon in the street?"

Ava nodded. "I had heard that. How awful that must

have been for him. He will have to carry that memory with him forever." She remembered her own memory that she carries around of her attempted suicide. As they talked her mind recalled the gas oven incident and she could practically feel the heat on her skin and the smell in her nostrils.

"Just awful!" Kira agreed. "I heard that your husband died. Sorry to hear that."

"Yes. Thank you. It has been tough with my seven children."

"Well, now that you are single and will have some money, I am sure you will do well!" Kira said excitedly.

*"What?"* Ava couldn't believe her ears.

"Yeah. Pretty people always do well, and now you are single with a few bucks!" Kira chuckled and gave a catty smirk.

Ava raised her eyebrows, showing her distaste for Kira's comment. "I really must get going."

"I must tell you—Caroline was by and asked for you. She wants to see you," added Kira.

"What?" She had met Caroline in Italy when Devon took her on that marvelous trip, and they had stayed at Caroline's family's villa. Ava recalled her as beautiful and rich. Her family had arranged for her to marry a man with a farm here. At first, Ava was excited to hear about her, but then she reflected on how her own life had taken a downward turn. She would be embarrassed to see Caroline—to let Caroline know that she had to marry an older man with whom she had another five children.

She'd be embarrassed for Caroline to learn she was so poor.

"I said she wants to see you," Kira repeated. "I'll get your address from Mr. Woods and give it to her."

Ava needed to get home to the children. She didn't have time to think about Kira giving Caroline her address. She waved her hand dismissively and hurriedly walked toward the trolley platform.

# CHAPTER TWO

———◆———

# Day-to-Day Living

About a week after the reading of Lady Tatum's will, Ava received a check for $2,000. She purchased a small two-story cottage on Poplar Street off Hyde Park Avenue. It was a pleasant residential area and within walking distance to the trolley platform. It had three small bedrooms so the older three girls could share one bedroom, and the others could share a second bedroom. She took the smallest bedroom for herself.

There was a partially finished room in the basement, and Trevor took that. He was maturing into a handsome young man, and his blond hair was turning light brown. He often reminded Ava of Alistar, his father. Even though she'd seen Alistar only a few times, they had made love. She realized now that she'd been foolish. She was happy she had her son, but being unwed and pregnant had disgraced her family. On top of that, she was considered a slut. It was tough to live in that spotlight, but she had no choice.

Trevor never asked about his real father. Ava waited for his questions, but they never came. Scott had been a real father to Trevor. When Ava married Scott, Trevor was about three years old, so she was sure that he must remember something. She eventually figured that Trevor must be satisfied with himself because he never asked about his biological father.

That weekend, Ava's two brothers came by to help her move out of the apartment and into her new house. Ava felt blessed that everything seemed well coordinated and that she didn't have to move in the dark to beat the landlord out of his money. That was a grueling process, and everyone was well familiar with it—they'd called it the "Paul Revere midnight move," as they had moved in that way so many times.

The children packed up their belongings and then walked a half mile to the new house. Carrying everything was physically difficult. They had to carry all the heavy metal bed parts down the street and then up the tiny wooden staircase, which was barely three feet wide. The first night, they managed to set up one metal bed, and the younger ones slept there; the others slept on the floor. They did manage to totally vacate their apartment. Ava's brother Tony swept and cleaned the apartment at dawn before he went home to his wife and children. Ava was thankful for her brothers, Jerry and Tony, who always seemed to be there for her.

Gradually, Ava and her children settled in to their new home.

One early summer afternoon, Ava was trimming the front bushes when a man appeared in front of her house. She continued trimming, not paying much attention to him. Her large straw hat partially obscured her view. Suddenly, she heard the man call, "Ava!"

His voice sounded vaguely familiar, but she couldn't think of where or when she had heard it. She glanced up, but the bright sunshine behind him blocked her view and created an aura around him. She slowly stood up, shielding her eyes, and looked at the man in disbelief. Her eyes narrowed, and her lips tightened—it was Alistar!

"Hello, Ava." He smiled almost sheepishly.

She felt frozen to the ground, but she glared at him and issued a cynical snort. She quickly did some soul searching as to how she should react. She'd thought he would never return.

His hand touched the brim of his hat in a polite greeting. "How are you?" he asked in a low tone.

She was still evaluating the situation and couldn't believe that it really was Alistar, but now she remembered his voice. She took a few steps toward him but remained silent. The bright sunshine continued to distort her view of him, and she couldn't positively identify him. She maintained her cold glare.

Suddenly, a jolt of adrenaline flowed through her body, causing her temperature, her blood pressure, and her anger to rise uncontrollably. *Yes, it's him!* Then, after another cynical snort, she sniped, "What are you doing here?"

He smiled and calmly answered, "to see you."

"You … you have no right to come here! You … you

abandoned your son and me! You forgot us! You left us alone! You left us in the cold to fend for ourselves, and now you return like nothing ever happened. You have a nerve! Go away! Don't ever come here again. I don't ever want to see you! I loathe you!" She turned and stomped back into the house. She knew if she caused a scene, the younger children would come out of the house, and she would have to explain what was going on here.

Once inside, she gave the front door a good slam. She was huffing and puffing from the encounter and had to catch her breath. The audacity of his coming here made her skin crawl with anger and resentment.

Things were going good for her and the children. She had survived Scott's death, and now, she and the children were happy; she wasn't financially struggling as she had done in her younger years. She was even viewed as a respectable widow now. She shuddered when she remembered having had kinky sex with a perverted landlord way back when she couldn't pay the rent, but now, she had a small home, thanks to Lady Tatum's gift for the care of Mary.

She also thought of Trevor, the result of her union with Alistar. Although Alistar never had tried to see their son, she assumed that was what he was seeking now.

Her emotions felt ambushed, and she had a strong sense that Alistar's return was not going to be good.

Still, as the following days went by uneventfully, and Ava's time was filled with the children's care and activities, she almost forgot about Alistar turning up in front of her house.

# CHAPTER THREE

# Employment

Ava took a good look at herself in the mirror. She knew it was time to figure out a way to survive. She was still an attractive woman, and all the childcare and physical care of Scott had kept her muscles in shape. She had breastfed all seven babies, but her breasts looked good and were large—she knew men were attracted to that feature.

When she pinned back her shoulder-length dark hair, she noticed a few gray hairs, but she used a bottle of magenta henna to color and blend the gray—the same technique that Cleopatra had used centuries ago, which amazed Ava. She noticed bags under her eyes but thought that they symbolized wear and tear after years of hard work. All in all, she figured she could clean herself up. She would have to get an outside job to survive. Trevor and Mary could run the household in her absence.

Ava had no real skills for the marketplace, but she had heard of a local factory, Raytheum, that made electronic parts, especially during wartime. It was located near the elevated train section just past Hyde Square in the center of Jamaica Plain, close enough for her to walk there.

Life had returned to a chaotic standard routine—a crazy norm for them, considering there were eight people in a three-bedroom bungalow. She knew that she needed to get a job to cover their living expenses. Everything was up to her now, as it had been since Scott's stroke, when he became disabled.

Her mind wandered as she thought of him. She did love him—to a point. He was the man who had taken her on, with two illegitimate children, which was a sin by anyone's standards. She had taken on him and his problems too. He was an illegal from England, who had probably deserted a wife and children there. She figured that she and Scott were even; it was a marriage of convenience.

She had heard there was an open job call that morning at eight o'clock. This was a sobering thought in the reality of her life. It seemed all too soon, but the day had come for her to go out into the labyrinth of the real world to get gainfully employed. She was not entirely prepared and almost had an anxiety attack, but she had to move forward; her children were depending on her. If she couldn't provide for her children, she realized that they could end up in an orphanage. She couldn't bear that thought.

She dressed neatly in a simple dress and put her dark hair up in a bun at the back of her head. She applied a little rouge to her cheeks and used just a dab of eyeshadow on her upper eyelids. She finished her facial portrait with red lipstick, which she'd heard was the current trend and signified an aura of ambition.

She left Trevor and Mary in charge; they always provided good care for the five younger ones. "The children are not to leave the house until I get home," she instructed them. "Most of them will sleep late anyway; they always do when it's summertime."

Off she went, even though she had the jitters and could feel slight perspiration on her body. She imagined that her nerves were crackling in response to her stress. As she walked, her mind wandered again to when she was alone with a baby and had to trade sex for rent with her disgusting landlord, Jose. She shivered as she thought of what she'd had to do with that perverted man. It was nauseating. He had taken advantage of her as a young woman. She couldn't stand the feel of his hands on her, especially on her naked skin in sensitive and private parts. Her stomach turned as she remembered how he had entered her vagina with his dirty prick and engaged to the point of a mammoth, pulsating climax within her. She couldn't believe how low she had gone when she was desperate. She hoped he was dead now—or at least suffering from some ill-fated misfortune!

She was thankful that she hadn't become pregnant by him, considering she got pregnant the first time she had intercourse with Alistar. She hadn't used a vinegar douche afterward, but that probably wouldn't have worked anyway. Alistar hadn't used a condom because he said it was "uncomfortable," and Jose was just an animal. She figured that maybe Jose had bad sperm, and that was why she didn't get pregnant by him. How awful that would have been.

She shook her head to clear her thoughts as she walked past Hyde Square and then down Call Street. She heard the noisy squeaking and squealing of the elevated trains above her head. *They could wake the dead*, she thought. She could see the electric bolts under the trains as they rumbled on the tracks.

She crossed the street diagonally to Forest Street and went all the way to the end, where the factory was located. There already was a long line of people, waiting. Soon the door opened, and everyone filed in quietly to a large room, where many chairs were set in parallel rows. Each person took a seat, and all seats soon were occupied. Ava looked behind her and still saw people entering. A man, who apparently was in charge, directed the extra people to line up against the back wall.

The economy was just coming out of the Great Depression, and now, there was a little flicker of hope of things improving in the United States.

At the front of the room, three men were seated, facing the crowd. One man spoke to the silent crowd. "We will pass out job applications. Please take one, then pass the rest to the next person in the row. Fill it out as best as you can. We will call you up individually to interview you."

*That was short and sweet*, Ava thought. She took her application from the pile and then passed the large pile to the next person. She could hear an undertone of voices—people asking for a pencil and others asking for help with the application. She surmised that some people were illiterate and couldn't read the application. She quickly pulled a pencil from her purse and filled out the application.

Everyone patiently waited for their turn to be interviewed. Ava waited for close to an hour before it was her turn.

She sat down across from the skinny man in the middle. She judged his age at about forty-five, as he had thinning gray hair and wrinkles on his face. He had an almost poultry look about him, with his skinny face and a beak of a nose. She was churning with anxiety and fear, but she forced herself to remain calm. Her body seemed to be getting used to the waves of fear and anxiety. She hoped she exuded an aura of serious, solemn demureness, and she straightened her shoulders to show good posture.

The man silently read her application and then said, "I see that you had some employment on a farm as a picker." His tone seemed to indicate disbelief. He hesitated as he continued to read, then said, "You worked as domestic help in Brookline many years ago. I also see that you had a long interval without any employment. Any reason for that?"

Ava knew that her answer would result in a make-it-or-break-it situation. She had to answer his question as clearly as she could, considering that she had only a rudimentary eighth-grade education. She desperately needed this job! She took a deep cleansing breath and answered from her heart. "Yes, sir, I was married, and my husband became ill. I was responsible for his total care until he recently died. I am a great worker, and I can do almost anything."

"Sorry about your husband. Could you work on a factory assembly line?" he asked. He solemnly looked at her with judgmental eyes that seemed to penetrate her mind and soul.

"Yes, sir! Most definitely. I can adapt easily, and I am a fast learner!" she exclaimed with energy and enthusiasm.

"Well, you can obviously read and write, which gives you an edge over some of the applicants here today. OK, I will give you a chance. We need someone who can read and follow directions carefully."

"Thank you, sir! You won't be sorry!" she exclaimed. She felt that she was glowing and had a smile from ear to ear.

"OK, you start Monday morning. Be here at seven o'clock, and we will train you. Once you're trained, you will work the second shift, which is three o'clock to eleven at night. Is that acceptable to you?"

"Of course! That is wonderful!" she answered with a brilliant smile.

Ava finally had a job in the real world. Although she was happy, she wasn't sure how she would care for the children now. This was a double-edged sword: she needed the money to support her family, but with those hours, her children would mostly be on their own. She thought of asking her elderly mother to mind the children, but her health was deteriorating. She dreaded the thought of what awaited her in the future but quickly realized that she had no other choice. She decided to have a positive attitude and move forward!

It was lunchtime when she returned home. The kitchen table was in disarray, covered with food remnants, spilled milk, and sticky fingerprints. As she viewed it with disgust, she decided to interpret it positively—at least the children had something to eat. As she started to clean up the mess, Julia chased Dalia into the kitchen. Dalia banged into the wall and fell backwards onto Julia. There was a symphony of crying, and Ava had to separate and comfort each child individually. She loved them dearly, and her heart was broken as she realized that she would have to work and not be around to care for them as much.

The three younger ones were dressed in their day clothes with their faces washed. Jenna and Samantha, her first two children with Scott, taking their turns in the bathroom. That left Shayne still in her pajamas, playing with an empty box in the corner. Ava quickly scooped her up in her arms and gave her kisses all over from side to side. Shayne let out a tidal wave of laughter as her mother gently rolled her around in her arms. Ava knew her children needed extra attention and love, especially since they had recently buried their father.

When everyone was finished, she took them out for a walk around the Arboretum Park that was about a half mile from their house. It was a gorgeous day, and she wanted to spend time with them. Soon, when she worked the evening shift, it would be difficult to find any quality time together. She also realized they needed time to grieve the loss of their father. She needed time to grieve too, but she knew her best course would be to plunge forward.

There was a small pond at the entrance, just beyond the immense wrought-iron gates of the park. A few ducks were sunning themselves on the edge of the pond. The children chased all the ducks back into the pond and then played ball on the rolling green grass. Soon, they were weary and returned home.

As they walked back to their home, Ava pondered how quickly their lives had changed. In a whirlwind of thoughts, she recollected burying Scott, an inheritance, a new home, and a new job. Everything was up to her.

On the following Monday morning, she left Trevor and Mary in charge at six o'clock so she would have enough time to walk to the Raytheum factory. With each step she took, she felt adrenaline and anxiety course through her blood as she wondered about her new job.

*If Amelia Earhart can fly a plane solo across an ocean,* Ava thought, *then I can do this! Heck, Amelia lived in Medford, only a few miles from here.*

She entered the building by the side door and saw about ten other new hires waiting there. Promptly, a man came down and called each person's name, then checked them off of a roster clipboard. He handed each of them preemployment papers and instructed them to write in their social security numbers. The social security tax law had just been implemented by President Roosevelt. It was to take money from a person's wages and put it into an account for that person's old-age retirement. Ava was skeptical of the tax, and no one knew if the concept would work. Still, it was a law now, so people had to abide by it. After all the paperwork was completed, the group followed the man into the main area of the factory.

It was a huge room with gigantic machinery. The apparatus almost reached to the third-story ceiling. An enormous wired window was located at the top of each wall to allow sunlight into the factory. There was a clamorous bang as the gears of the equipment contracted and retracted in a synchronized manner. Multiple conveyor belts branched off the main apparatus and down to workstations. As the items reached each station on the conveyor belt, an uproarious noise was emitted after the metal parts were fused. Then followed a smaller, gun-like thudding noise. A different function was performed at each workstation along the conveyor belt, and when it was finished, it was automatically pushed to the next workstation. Everything functioned on a fast-paced timer, which meant that the person at each workstation only had seconds to do what was required before the product was moved on. It was difficult to listen to the constant loud bang.

Ava assumed the noise occurred to let out pressure from whatever had been joined. It did hurt her ears, and she knew that it would be a difficult environment for her—or anyone—to work in. The factory was made of thick brick, and it seemed the noises just rumbled and rattled off the walls, causing the sound waves to bounce back into the large room.

The manager had to talk loudly to be heard over

the thunderous machinery. "First, what we do here is confidential, and you are not to talk to anyone about which products are manufactured. Second, you will work with a partner for a few days, and then you will be expected to work on your own on the assembly line. Third, make sure that you ask all your questions in the next three days so that you can independently perform your job on the assembly line. You will be alone thereafter."

Ava was assigned to work with a woman who was about her age, and she intently followed everything the woman said and did.

The woman explained, "We make glass tubes, and we put a wire in each tube so that it heats up to cause an electrical charge. This is the beginning of a radio tube assembly line. These new radio tubes are the beginning of the evolution from the D-battery radios that often fail and leak. The two-inch, cylinder-shaped, glass vacuum tube will come from another assembly line on the conveyer belt. You pick it up and place the thin, flat conducting wire inside the tube at the tip. It's important that the wire, or filament, is attached just right to allow the electrical current to flow through the tube and make the connection. Next, you put the tube back on the conveyor belt, and it will go to the next station, where it will be sealed to a base without oxygen so that a negative- and positive-ion magnetic field will be created. This magnetic field creates heat and conducts energy. In essence, the first light bulb was invented by Thomas Edison in 1880, and what we are producing is similar but used for radios."

Ava knew that she was a part of a new technology

and was proud of it. The radio was revolutionizing media routes, as newspapers were the only other source of information. It was an American pastime to gather in the living room and listen to the radio.

After three long days of instruction, Ava was on her own. Surprisingly, the factory was relatively quiet, even though there were many people at different stations. The only chatter was from the conveyor belts. Everyone worked intently and individually; they all were grateful to be employed.

# CHAPTER FOUR

# On the Way to Work

One day as Ava was walking to work along Hyde Park Avenue, a car stopped, and a man leaned over to ask her if she wanted a ride. It was Alistar!

She panicked when she saw him. She knew he had been from Mystic Seaport, Connecticut, and if he still lived there, he was a long way from his home. Then she became furious and yelled, "Get away from me! I don't want you near me or my children!" She walked faster down the street, but he followed along, his vehicle at a crawl.

"Look, I'm sorry!" he yelled out the window.

Ava maintained her cold attitude, even though her porcelain skin was now crimson with anger!

"Please get in the car so we can talk," Alistar said.

"Never! I said I don't want you near me or my children!" She stopped and turned toward his car. When she spoke again, there was an avalanche of emotion in her voice. "You took advantage of me and used me for your own pleasure. I never heard from you again, not even after I had your son over seventeen years ago! Oh, excuse me, you told your friend Tom that you couldn't help me because you were with a rich politician's daughter in Connecticut! How was your life? Mine was miserable, and we barely had anything to eat! You have no idea how difficult things were for us! Just a little support from time to time would have been appreciated. Oh no, not you, who was too busy enjoying life! You blatantly abandoned us! You need to do some soul searching for your actions, mister! You are the epitome of stupidity! Now leave us alone, or I will call the police the next time you come around!"

"Ava, please listen to me!" he said, shifting uncomfortably in the car seat. "Yes, I married Margaret, but I was also still enlisted in the service, and I became disabled due to the explosion of an underwater mine."

Ava lowered her eyes but said, "Well … sorry to hear that." Then she became overcome by grief and anger, and shook her head almost uncontrollably as she shouted, "What the hell did you do to me and your son? We were prisoners of constant disadvantages—never had the advantages you had! We had no food at times. I had to pick through trash cans to find food. I was assaulted while doing that! I had to do awful things to keep a roof over our heads—everyone thought that I was promiscuous and took advantage of me! Tell me that is not a prison! Sorry about your suffering for survival, but we had our own!" Now, tears spilled onto her cheeks as she stood like a stone statue but breathing heavily as she tried to exhale decades of anger and resentment.

He turned the engine off and got out of the car. He approached her with trepidation. Slowly, he raised his hands and gently rubbed her upper arms in an expression of reassuring comfort and condolence. With genuine compassion, he glanced at her and then softly said, "I know my abandonment can never be justified, and you have every right to hate me—shush, shush. Please get into the car, and I will take you wherever you want to go."

She raised her head up and glared at him in reproach. The turmoil that she had housed for decades was running like a turbo engine within her. Now, her chest was heaving as tears flowed, and she felt like a whirlwind was around her. Her tone was defiant when she said, "I trusted you once, and look where it got me." She restrained her impulse to push him into the street.

He directly met her gaze and nodded, clearly ashamed, but he didn't remove his hands from her upper arms; he maintained his cautious embrace. "Your accusations are all true. I have no right to be here, but I was hoping you could see it in your heart to forgive me."

Ava blinked away tears as she gradually gained control of herself. With a quivering smile, her lips parted, and she venomously replied, "No!"

Her tone and stiff body language let him know he should step backward, and he fell silent. It was as if time had stopped.

She read his face and knew that her scalding comment had forced her enemy to retreat. With a gleam in her eyes and an air of triumph, she dismissed him by saying, "I have to go now. My boss is a stickler for punctuality." She walked straight ahead, as if she had never veered off course. She remained stone-faced and did not look back at him, but she knew he could only concede to her. She crossed the street as if nothing had happened. She didn't notice when he drove past her.

The summer ended, and the children who were old enough went to school at St. Mary's, which was a short walk down Huntington Avenue. When Ava enrolled the children there, the Catholic school didn't charge her. She assumed it was the church's charitable contribution to her and her situation. Julia was only three, so Ava cared for her during the day. Mary and Trevor were home by 2:20, and this gave Ava enough time to walk to her job. After work, she took the bus home for safety reasons, as her shift ended at eleven.

Everything seemed to be going well, until one evening when she returned home to find police cars at the house. Instinctively, she knew it was for her children. As Ava exited the bus, she could see all the commotion and became frantic to learn what had occurred.

She approached a policeman who was coming out of her house. "What's going on, Officer? This is my house. Could you explain, please?"

The large burly policeman explained, "Apparently, a neighbor saw Julia—is she your little girl?—on the second floor, leaning out a window. Luckily, the neighbor ran across the street and talked the child back in."

"Julia's my daughter," Ava said.

"Where were you?"

"I was at work, sir," Ava said. She could feel herself getting nervous and her face turning red. "My husband died, and I leave my two older children in charge."

"Well, put a bar across the window." His voice softened a bit. "I'd advise you to get an adult in the apartment when you work."

Ava could tell that he was empathetic to her single-parent situation. She felt blessed that getting an adult to stay there was the only thing he advised. She did take it seriously. As old as her mother was, she would have to mind the children during the week.

After the police left, Ava told the children, "You must be careful and be aware that there is a danger of falling out of a window." Once they were back in bed, she also thanked the neighbor for intervening in the situation.

Ava soon realized that her paycheck would not cover all the household expenses—utilities and food for the family. Mary took it well and did what she was told. Soon, she found employment at a string factory in Boston.

Ava tried to keep Trevor in high school as this was his last year, and she knew education was best spent on a boy. He would be expected to be the breadwinner for his family someday. She assumed Mary would marry, so she didn't necessarily need an education. A few months later, however, Ava realized that Trevor had to quit school and get a job to contribute to the family expenses.

One Saturday, as Ava was folding laundry, the doorbell rang. She opened the door and immediately recognized Caroline. "Oh my God! How are you?"

They embraced each other with smiles and laughter.

"We must talk!" Ava said. "Come in. Follow me to the kitchen, and I'll make some tea." As Caroline followed her, Ava quickly said, "I apologize for the muddled mess. With seven children, the house is always cluttered with toys and their other things."

"Oh, no problem. I have three children of my own," Caroline said in her Italian accent. "It is so good to see you. I've wanted to connect with you since I came to America, but I didn't know where you were."

Ava served the tea as she whispered, so as not to be overheard by the children, "Yes, well, it hasn't been easy. I became pregnant by Devon, and then his wife returned."

Caroline nodded. "I did hear that."

"So you know that when Jane returned, she was pregnant by some old boyfriend. Apparently, she threatened to destroy the family business and name if Devon didn't take her back. She wasn't going to let him see Brendon either! He wanted to take my baby so he and Jane could raise her. Of course, I didn't allow that. I knew Jane was a fraud. I had a tough time dealing with things. My father arranged a marriage for me to a man named Scott. We had five children together. He recently died."

"Wow! So you were practically constantly pregnant," Caroline said. "Babies are wonderful, though. They are like an extension of ourselves and our lives. They give us purpose."

"Yes, for sure." Ava purposely didn't mention that she had tried to commit suicide when she was pregnant with Devon's baby and ended up in a mental facility for depression. "After Scott died, I had no income. It was like a fairy tale come true when Lady Tatum left me money."

"Yes, I heard that too," Caroline said.

"Well, what about you?" asked Ava.

"Things are good. I married Michael, the son of the man who owned the farm that you knew of. We have a nice house in Dedham. He is in the Mafia," Caroline said nonchalantly and in almost one breath.

Ava could barely conceal her shock and surprise, but she didn't say anything.

"I had no idea what I was getting into when my father arranged the marriage when we were in Italy," Caroline said.

"So, what is your life like?" Ava asked. Although she was still totally flabbergasted by what Caroline had just revealed, she tried to be objective and not show any emotion.

"I am scared for my children and myself. Michael goes out at night, and I think he gets money from business owners. He returns and looks like he has been in a fight. I don't know what to do." Caroline lowered her head onto her crossed arms and cried.

Ava reached over and gave her a comforting hug. *Her plight is worse than hers,* she thought. "If there is anything I can do, let me know."

Caroline wiped away her tears and gathered up her

belongings. "I must go now. I wanted to see you, and I am glad I did."

After she left, Ava thought again that as bad as her own life was, Caroline's was even worse.

# CHAPTER FIVE

# Alistar's Fate

The USS *Donovan* had sailed out of port in Boston Harbor, just after the Great War ended and before Ava could tell Alistar that she was carrying his child.

The ship was scheduled to go to Virginia and then down to the naval base in Key West, Florida. The large warship was to be decommissioned and ultimately destroyed in Key West.

Alistar still had active-duty time to finish in order to receive an honorable discharge. He was very proud to fight for his country. He felt it was not only his duty but an honor. He would be stationed in England and then Turkey in the Black Sea, as part of the effort to dismantle enemy military bases and their ships to secure peace in the world. Another purpose was to rebuild areas where bombs had destroyed cities and the countryside. The United States took on a large undertaking and effort, with many facets to reuniting and restructuring the damage that the war had caused.

When the *Donovan* docked off the coast of Virginia, Alistar was allowed to return home to Connecticut for a two-week period. Everyone was celebrating and jubilant about the end of the war. Soon, Alistar would be departing for Europe, and his tour was deemed indefinite—he had no return date back to the States. When his fiancée discovered he was still going to be on active duty, they decided to have the wedding earlier than originally planned.

He had not been on land since he was in Boston. He played over and over in his mind that first sexual adventure with Ava. He had been a virgin, but that had all changed with her. Even though he didn't see her much while he was in port, he did care for her. He knew if he hadn't been engaged to Margaret, he would have been madly in love with Ava.

He couldn't wait to get home. There would be many festivities—a welcome home party, an engagement party, and then, finally, the wedding. He also was looking forward to having intercourse!

He had a long time to think as he took the train from Pennsylvania to New York; then he transferred to another train in New York to Boston. That train stopped in Bridgeport, Connecticut, where he would be picked up for the last part of his journey, home to Mystic Seaport.

As he got off the train, he could barely hear over loud train whistles. He was tired and exhausted from the long ride; he'd not gotten much sleep in the uncomfortable berth. He could see Margaret standing at the station in her fur coat, waving her white-gloved hand high in the air toward him. He was ecstatic to see her. She looked marvelous—blonde hair, her high cheekbones, blue eyes, long eyelashes, and dazzling smile! She stood with his brother, David. Alistar ran to her, and they wildly embraced in a lover's lock and twirl. It felt good to have his hands on her. He spun her around and around and then planted her feet back on the ground and gave his brother a quick lean-over hug with a handshake.

Margaret gave him another hug and a long kiss. She met his gaze and whispered, "I have missed you so much!" They stared at each other, inches apart, as her words hung in the air. "You have lost weight," she said, pulling back as her eyes went up and down his frame.

"Yes, I have," he answered. "You look magnificent! The same way that I remembered you."

"Well, her fine cooking will beef you up again, I am sure," David interjected. "In the meantime, let's get you home. Mom is waiting to see you too."

They left the station and went to their house, a period-detailed colonial with a fine American flag flying over the front porch. Alistar paused for a moment, then slowly walked down the bluestone pathway and climbed the six stairs to the wrap-around veranda as he felt a flood of emotion. He was so grateful to be home. He wiped his feet as he wiped away his tears.

Margaret noticed his weariness and took his arm in a comforting embrace. "It's OK, honey," she said softly. "You're home now."

The front door opened, and his mother was standing there. She greeted him in a long and intense embrace, followed by jubilant kisses. "My baby is home safe and sound!" she exclaimed.

He passed through the front foyer, where the stairs were constructed in a right angle that flowed to the second story. There was a landing about eight steps up that looked like a statesman's balcony. The hardwood floors gleamed as they caught the sunshine coming in the large windows. The sunshine beamed on the exact place where Alistar jumped up on the landing. There, he proceeded to loudly announce, "Hear ye, hear ye! All listen, as Alistar has returned home!" His announcement ended with a tip of his hat.

Afterward, they all entered the dining room that was off the foyer, where there were trays of food to welcome him home. He saw the large dining room table that they all sat around and had many good holiday and meal gatherings. This was such a wonderful, welcoming reminder of his life before he had left for war.

His mother announced the itinerary: a small welcome-home reception the following evening at their house and then an engagement party on Saturday evening at Margaret's. There was chaos as the engagement party and wedding were moved up so that the two of them could be married before he had to return to duty. He was scheduled to be overseas for at least a year.

Alistar was fatigued from the war and from traveling. Shortly thereafter, he retired to his childhood bedroom to rest.

The next night, the welcome-home party was catered at their house. It was small and intimate. His old buddies attended. Whoever was still in the military wore their dress uniforms, which was a reminder of what the country had just endured. These were crazy times, as the country was still actively securing post-war issues, and not everyone was out of the service.

The engagement party was at Margaret's family house. When Alistar arrived, he paused to look at the stately columns in front of her house. It seemed that the columns were almost saluting him. He was so proud to be in the military and defending the freedom of the United States—his United States. It was a good time, as everyone was celebrating the end of the war and worshipping the living soldiers who had returned. Of course, there was also grief, as there had been many casualties. Every American was respectful of those grieving families whose family member was not returning. It was known as the "ultimate sacrifice."

Margaret's house was packed, as her father was a state representative. Alistar did not know most of the people, but his future father-in-law, Joseph Peters took him around and introduced him to everyone. Of course, Alistar would never remember anyone, as he was so overloaded with the new names and faces. There was plenty of food, waiters serving drinks, decorations, and a live band for the festivities.

Finally, Mr. Peters left. Then there was a drum roll, and he reappeared on the large staircase. Now Margaret stood beside him, dressed elegantly in a shimmering silver, low-cut, tightly fitted sequined gown. Long diamond earrings hung from her ears and matched the diamond necklace around her neck. It seemed that the diamond jewelry was alive, as it flowed together around her and dipped into her cleavage. The jewelry gracefully swayed from side to side with every movement she made. Her blonde hair and blue eyes caught everyone's attention as she slowly walked down the staircase on her father's arm.

Alistar was at the bottom of the stairs, and he let out a small gasp when he saw how stunning she looked.

Mr. Peters announced, "I am so happy that my beautiful daughter is marrying a man who has served and continues to serve this country. I feel great despair that my daughter is leaving me, but I feel even greater inspiration that she is joining Alistar in marriage. I know this union will bring complete happiness to both of them."

Alistar extended his arm to Margaret at that point, and they kissed. "I take Margaret, and you need not despair, as I know that we will be happy together."

"Yes, and make me a lot of grandchildren!" added Mr. Peters in a jovial tone.

Everyone raised their champagne glasses to toast the couple.

Ten days later, Alistar and Margaret were scheduled to be married. Their itinerary was to leave after the weekend, which barely gave them time for a quick honeymoon to the White Mountains in New Hampshire before he was to leave.

On the day of the wedding, Alistar was waiting at the church with his brother, David, who would serve as best man. It was a little white stucco church on the coast of Mystic Seaport. Inside, one large gold cross was at the altar, and two long stained-glass windowpanes were in the wall behind the altar. Simple paintings of the Stations of the Cross were on the side walls. Rows of deep, rich mahogany pews with highly shellacked finishing caught the colors of the stained glass reflecting on them. A white carpet was down the middle of the rows of pews for the bride to walk down. An extravagant display of bridal flowers made the simple church almost come alive. There were dozens of large bouquets of multicolored daisies, orchids, roses, and carnations at the altar floor. On the end of the pews were smaller matching bouquets within a sheer netting, wrapped in brightly colored ribbons.

The ocean was nearby, and they could hear the waves retreat and then return. There were a few large elm trees on the property, and a wisteria-covered white wooden arch with a trellis on each side strategically placed with the ocean as a backdrop. Picture-perfect hibiscus bushes with pink blossoms were in the forefront of each trellis, which enhanced the arch and color of the wisteria— nature's bountiful beauty.

The wedding march started, and all the guests rose from their pews. A bridesmaid walked down the aisle, and then came Margaret, on her father's arm. She looked gorgeous in her white satin gown, which fit the hourglass-shaped curves of her sexy body. The gown had a simple white-lace trim on the low neckline—which highlighted her cleavage. The same white trim bound and encircled the edge of the sheer sleeves, and the border extremity of the train. She wore a simple strand of pearls around her neck and a tiara that had a full finger-length white veil in the back. A smaller version of the veil covered her face. When she arrived at the altar, her father turned, lifted her veil, and kissed her goodbye. Alistar stepped into Mr. Peters's place and took Margaret's arm as they both turned and proceeded to the altar. Then they faced the priest as a couple to be united.

After the priest's sermon to honor each other, they exchanged wedding rings. Next came saying "I do," which they each repeated. Finally, the priest introduced them to the wedding guests as man and wife. They turned and faced the crowd. Alistar bent Margaret back slightly to engage in a passionate kiss. Then all the guests stood and applauded!

Alistar took Margaret's hand, and they ran down the white carpet between the pews to the doorway of the church. The photographer had them stop there, and he took photographs of them with the church in the background.

All the guests came out to hug and congratulate the newly married couple. Plenty of rice was thrown at them as they walked away from the church.

The photographer took them to the picturesque arch, where he took more photographs with the roaring ocean in the background.

Her father had a limousine waiting for the couple that took them to a large hall for the wedding reception. Dancing, eating, and music comprised the rest of the evening.

Alistar and Margaret soon left the festivities to start their honeymoon. They had limited time for their honeymoon and were eager to consummate their marriage.

It took six hours for them to drive to Mount Washington in New Hampshire. Alistar wanted to drive up the mountain, as it was considered the first man-made tourist attraction. It even had a cog railway that originally was said to go to the moon, as it was so high in the sky. His dream was to see the view from the top. He made a reservation in a hotel with a picturesque view that was geologically wedged on a plateau just to the side of the mountain.

Alistar and Margaret were in their own world. After they checked into the hotel, they went to their room, where he lifted her into his strong arms and gave her a soft kiss. He cradled her in his arms and carried her over the threshold to the honeymoon suite. He did a swift backward kick with one leg and pushed the door closed, even as he still concentrated on kissing his bride. It was about five feet to the large bed, and he gently placed her on the bed. They both were feeling woozy from the effects of all the champagne toasts at the reception, combined with the long, tiring ride. He continued to kiss her; then he ran his hand gently through her hair as he stopped kissing her. Quickly, he ran his hand down her dress to gain access to her leg. He touched her knee and massaged his way up between her thighs to feel the outline of her anatomy at her apex between her labia. He slowly continued circlelike finger wandering until he reached the edge of her panty line, where he went under to explore the fine pubic goods in long, gentle, teasing strokes. Swiftly, he inserted his middle finger into her vagina. He could feel the lubricating warmth and tight structure. He couldn't control himself and quickly stood upright, unzipped his pants, and briskly removed them, revealing his totally erect penis, ready for action and release.

Margaret lifted her buttocks and removed her panties. She vigorously placed her hand on his penis and started a stroking action. Her dress was up, exposing her naked hips and pelvis.

Alistar had a sudden flashback of Ava as she had readied herself for him. He entered Margaret, and she was tight. He had to push himself into her body. He even had to stop a few times, not to push too hard and make another entry hole in her anatomy. It was a tough penetration for him; he was expecting more pleasure and ecstasy. He quickly finished his male strokes within her vagina, and when he finally released himself, he almost called her Ava.

A crater-shaped pool of water had formed from the melting snowpacks just outside their room. They could hear gallons of rumbling water run past their window to the river below. It created a thick curtain of misty fog that blocked most visibility. The air was thick, and the whole atmosphere felt cold and damp.

They slept together, as lovers do, but somehow, Alistar's thoughts were on a vision of Ava. He just couldn't get her out of his mind or control his thoughts of her.

They spent the next day sightseeing and enjoying the picturesque scenery of the mountains. They drove to the top of the mountain and found a small information site and an observatory station that took scientific data on wind, weather, and altitude. Alistar was totally engrossed in the information, but Margaret was bored with it. She did enjoy the view and the shadows of the mountains on the larger mountain ranges. The drive down was close to a catastrophic experience, as the road went around and around the enormous mountain. Alistar had to ride his brakes so that the car wouldn't go off the mountainside. Margaret was silent and scared, as she could smell and see the smoke coming from the brakes. Her hands shook uncontrollably, and that matched her inner nerves! When they reached the Kancamagus Highway, they were thankful to be off the mountain. They returned to their room for rest and another sexual odyssey.

Alistar wanted to see Franconia Notch, where a river gorge traveled through a mountain. It was stunning to see the natural beauty that Mother Nature had created. Later that evening, they enjoyed a nice dinner at a small Italian restaurant that overlooked the Saco River. The following day, on their way back to Connecticut, they stopped in the coastal towns of Maine's Kennebunkport, Wells, and York.

When they returned, they spent their remaining time at Margaret's house. After Alistar relaxed, it was soon time for him to return to duty and to go overseas.

It took him a full five days to get to London. He was to stay there for six months and then go to Turkey.

While in Turkey, he wrote to Margaret almost every day. They exchanged passionate letters with each other. No words could describe how they truly missed each other as a new couple.

The Turkish countries' cultural traditions of dress, food, and religion were strange to him, and he couldn't understand or speak the Arabic language. Routinely, he viewed the devastation from the war and reflected on how the whole country seemed to be bombed and blown apart.

Shell-like structures stood where homes had been and people previously resided. It was sad. Even though he had defended his country, viewing the destruction of the effects of war brought a sick feeling to his stomach as he surveyed the bombed areas. A lot of rebuilding was going to be necessary. Meanwhile, the civilians remained diligent and tried to pick up their lives and move forward. He was glad that he would be transferred to France, where he would be participating in making a large communication tower. Everywhere, there were numerous land and naval bases being disestablished.

One day, he received a letter from his naval friend Tom, with whom he had served on the USS *Donovan*. Tom wrote about the two women that they had met while in Boston and how the one Alistar had been with was supposedly pregnant with his baby. Alistar couldn't believe it. Ava was pregnant with his baby, after just the one time that they'd had intercourse? He played back the memory of the time they were together; it was his first time at sex. Astoundingly, if he was to compare Ava to Margaret, he certainly enjoyed having intercourse with Ava more. He thought maybe it was because it was his first time; he assumed for both of them.

His wife, Margaret, was more like a cold fish in bed with him. He knew his thoughts were probably clouded, as they didn't get much time together, and everything was so rushed because he had to get back to naval duty. Maybe they just needed time to synchronize with each other's bodies.

He wrote a letter back to Tom, indicating that he would not be able to help Ava. How did he know if Ava actually was pregnant with his baby anyway? She might have been with other men.

Shortly after he wrote that letter to Tom, he received a letter from Margaret, telling him that she was due to have a baby in six months! They hadn't had much time for sex, yet here she was, pregnant too. He was overjoyed by the news! It was tough, though, as he was thousands and thousands of miles away from her, with no real timetable for returning home.

Time continued slowly for Alistar, as he was in France for a full year. He was granted time off but there was never enough time to return home, as that trip could take multiple days each way. He managed to be content with relaxing and seeing the French sights that were not bombed during the war. His favorite icon was the Eiffel Tower, which managed to survive the war. He was intrigued by it, as it had a temperature-control station at the top and a scientific wind tunnel at the base. Radio transmissions of German communications were intercepted from it, giving an edge to the French that the Germans had planned to bomb it. They also learned the names of some spies. It was the tallest structure in Paris. To Alistar, it was not only an artistic marvel but a relic of the Great War, with the true function of protecting its country.

Midway through his time in France, Margaret wrote that she had a baby girl, and she had named her Allison; her nickname would be Allie. She felt this was the female version of Alistar. She enclosed a sweet baby picture of her, which he carried in his wallet. He looked at the picture at least twice a day, as he missed them so much. The photograph signified his belonging to his life and home in America.

# CHAPTER SIX

## Tragedy and Rehabilitation

Alistar's next assignment took him to the Baltic Sea, where the United States was to either dismantle ships or sell them in order to dispose of the German fleet.

They had been on this assignment for a good eight months, and Alistar was getting very homesick. While traveling at sixty-five knots, the large ship's rippling effect ignited the horns of a mine that lay hidden in the depths of the ocean floor. The ship immediately exploded, as if a torpedo had struck it from the bottom. Consecutive loud blasts caused flying debris and sky-high flames that created flumes of displaced water upward to the sky. The wave blasts were so intense that it triggered other pressurized oxygen pockets of water-fueled flames to explode as the ship began to sink. Then, it just kept firing, upward and onward like fireworks!

The men didn't have time to prepare, and many died right there and then. Some men were blown from the ship and landed in the water. It was as if the large warship became airborne and went ballistic as it catapulted large pieces of metal debris, causing enormous waves that fueled the blast winds. There was turmoil in the sky, with constant flying objects, loud noise, agonizing screams, and a firewall of flames. Metal debris continued to splinter the sky. The repetitive rippling effects of the waves propelled more fire and water turmoil. Many men were injured and drowning.

From a distance, there was a silhouette of a fire that engulfed the sky, with a water flume consisting of explosive gasses, fueled by human life. Soon, the ship sank—like the darkness when a stage curtain comes down at the end of a play. The ship seemed to have been swallowed whole. Then, there was quiet.

Alistar's body was slammed up against a fragmented metal wall of the ship. He was unconscious but was one of the lucky ones, as he floated face up in the cold, murky, rocking water. The Baltic Sea could be compared to an angry green monster that swallowed everything whole.

About a year later, Alistar awoke from an intense coma with a cloudy and foggy mind. His vision was severely blurred. He couldn't remember what had happened and didn't know where he was. He couldn't even remember his name.

A nurse noticed his alertness and ran to his side. She spoke in French, and Alistar didn't understand her. She gently pushed his head back down on the pillow, which he understood, as he was suffering from an extreme pounding in his head. He had explosions of headache waves that just wouldn't stop. His eardrums seemed to be bulging, which caused even more excruciating pain. He gave the nurse a silent nod and rested his head on the pillow. He felt like every blood vessel, artery, and vein in his brain was loose and sloshing adrift in his cranium.

Months passed, and his mind pieced together the ferocity of the ordeal, although he couldn't quite remember anything else. He was told that only a handful of men survived, and he was one of the lucky ones. Alistar didn't feel lucky; he suffered great depression, knowing that he was among the living. Soon, his memory started to come back to him. He would think of his life before the accident. He tried to picture Margaret and their daughter, but this did not comfort him, as his depression ran deep. Also, he remained cynical that the Lord had allowed him to live while many others perished. Self-absorption and remorse weighed heavily on him as he tried to understand his fate. His eyes were ringed with dark circles, reflecting his sadness and trauma. He felt so alone and worn out. His stoic personality was fortified by bitterness, fear, and anger that he was forced to absorb because of being a survivor, along with intense regret and guilt that he was still breathing on this earth while his shipmates had perished.

He remained bedridden for a very long time. Soon, he discovered he had lost a leg. He was shocked by his altered body image, which created another tidal wave of anxiety and depression. After the physical ailments were addressed, his psychic being needed healing. He spent many hours in therapy with a psychiatrist who told him that he had suffered "polytrauma," meaning that he had many injuries. Constant headaches and blurred vision continued to plague him, which the psychiatrist attributed to the massive concussion he had suffered. Alistar believed his physical symptoms were the result of survivor's guilt. The horrors of war would play out as if on an imaginary screen in front of his eyes. He remembered being patriotic and so proud to defend his country. Now, he suffered from anxiety and depression, which hindered his ability to adapt to a prosthetic leg. Many hours went into physical therapy for him to learn to walk again. It took months for him to even accept that he had lost his limb. He stayed in bed as he succumbed to his depression.

First, he was made to sit on the side of the bed and dangle his legs. This was to help stabilize his blood pressure so he wouldn't feel woozy or dizzy. He felt that he was always dizzy, though. The medical staff next introduced him to a wheelchair. For Alistar, the wheelchair signified the reality of his doomed situation. He viewed the wheelchair as a terrible enemy and compared it to the sides of a naval ship that contained him, but now, the shiny metal sides of the wheelchair imprisoned his entire body. Just the sight of the metal sides of the wheelchair would trigger his anxiety. How his life had changed!

He continued to suffered from blurred vision and headaches, which delayed his progress even more. The doctors told him that his symptoms were a long-term effect of the concussion to his head. At times, the medical staff observed him sitting in his wheelchair, facing a corner and softly crying. Defeat engulfed him in a tangled matrix of thoughts as he suffered from a hungry guilt that gnawed at him and swallowed his existence.

Ultimately, he was faced with reality of another amputation surgery. Gangrene had set in his amputated leg, resulting in the need to remove more of his leg higher up. The nurses changed the dressings three times a day, and he often would look away from their medical ministrations, in denial of his reality. Days later, when the sutures were to be removed, and all the doctors surrounded his bed, he continued to distance himself. He asked for extra morphine to decrease the pain of the manipulation of the severed bone and tissues in his shortened leg. In his mind, he wanted the morphine to decrease the mental pain that plagued him, more so than the physical pain. He eventually had multiple surgeries on his leg, as gangrene necrosis kept creeping into the vascular areas. As time went on, he never attempted to touch or explore the shortened surface of his leg.

When it was time to be fitted for a prosthetic leg, Alistar sat in the wheelchair and felt the skin on the bottom of his missing leg, which was below the knee. It felt smooth and taut at the same time. He thought he was holding a small bomb in his hand—it was a bomb in his mind! He envisioned explosions going off in his head as he touched what was left of his leg. After he felt the bottom of his stump, he ran his hand over the healed scar tissue. It was not a totally foreign scar, and he soon learned to accept it. This was his new body, and as limited as it was, he was going to have to live with it! Still, he internally ached over his exterior.

The orthopedic physicians fitted his leg stump by carefully measuring it. About a month later, they returned with an almost toy-looking wooden leg. It had netting and a suction cap on the end. Straps came from the anterior portion, which would make the attachment to his stump. The wooden portion of the leg was heavy, and then it tapered down to a posterior metal rod. Finally, at the bottom, was a wooden foot that would fit into his shoe. At first, he had no reaction, as he was in shock. The therapist attached the leg to his stump. Next the therapist, the doctor, and his nurse circled around him and locked his wheels in order to have him stand—as a man that he once was. Standing was empowering, and he knew that he could overcome this trauma. It took months to learn how to walk with the prosthetic leg though.

When the therapist strapped the leg on with the suction cup, this caused friction and discomfort on the stump. Gradually, Alistar practiced walking between metal bars. He could hold himself up with his strong biceps, which aided and advanced his therapy so he could walk and be independent. His steps were very slow and small in the beginning. At first, he had to hold on with all his body strength, but soon, he built up his muscles and could stand straight and walk as if he still had his own leg.

Alistar built up tolerance, as he found that walking with the prosthetic leg took even more energy and strength from within to maneuver simple steps. Sometimes, when he was in bed, he would wake up and think his left leg was still attached, as he felt pain in it. The doctor called that "phantom pain." He would try to get out of bed in the morning, forgetting that his leg was gone, only to fall on the floor.

He received countless letters from Margaret and his daughter who wanted to visit him, but he told them not to come. He wasn't ready for them to see him. He constantly made up excuses. Margaret frequently sent pictures of Allie and her, but Alistar could not bear seeing her; he felt he was less than human with the loss of his leg. Not only was his mind and emotional being not ready for them, but he was having a challenging time accepting his changed body image; he felt less of a man.

Unexpectedly, he developed temporary hallucinations, in which an imaginary blast would explode right in front of him. He would go into a fearful trance, perspire heavily, and his muscles would tighten up. After a few years, the visual hallucinations subsided but were replaced with auditory hallucinations, in which he heard the voices of the men who were on the ship. Alistar was sure definitely existed, although he claimed to the psychiatrist that he was aware that they were not real. There were no effective medications to treat his condition, which the doctors called shell- shocked, but vitamin B was being researched as therapeutic. Alistar took the vitamin, although he was not sure if it helped or if he was getting used to his latent mental and physical recuperation. He wrote numerous letters to Margaret and Allie, but he never mentioned his medical conditions; he kept them in the dark. Evasiveness became second nature to him, and he would never commit to definite plans for a reunion with them. He kept everyone at a distance.

When he was offered a desk job at the French Embassy as a naval liaison for the United States, he accepted the position and spent another five years there. He maintained correspondence with Margaret and his daughter. Finally, he agreed to let them visit him in France.

# CHAPTER SEVEN

# Getting Back with Margaret

Alistar stood on shore, waiting for the large passenger ship to anchor. The ship was magnificent, with multiple decks and strategically placed portholes on the sides. It was bright white with red circles around each porthole to make it stand out. A red line continued from the bow to the stern along the side of the ship. The ship was so shiny that it appeared to have a coat of lacquer on it that caught the sunshine and made it sparkle.

Alistar was full of anxiety and impatience as he watched the crew painstakingly align the plank for the passengers to exit to the dock. As he stood on the shore, the image of his ship blowing up from the mine blast flashed before his eyes. He quickly pulled himself together, dispelling his negative thoughts, and reassured himself that this was a joyful occasion. Still, seeing Margaret again was challenging. This thought alone caused him anxiety.

It had been over a decade since he had seen her. He

wasn't sure he would even recognize her. He was conscious of his prosthetic leg, even though he was confident that he had incorporated it into his appearance rather well, to the point that he believed it was hardly noticeable. Sometimes, he would take longer to go from a sitting position to a standing position because it took extra strength. He needed to make sure he balanced his total body properly so he could stand correctly. When he moved to the left, on the side of the heavy wooden leg, he would almost skip a small step, resulting in a slight limp. He felt put together enough, though, and brought himself to the reality that his family needed to reunite. Together, they would have to work out their future.

He carefully watched the passengers disembark. Then he saw someone who looked like Margaret, with a young girl trailing behind her. *That must be them*, he thought. Margaret wore a big white-straw picture hat with a black ribbon tied in a bow on the front, which matched her black sheath-style dress. The dress followed the curves of her body. He noticed that she had put on weight over the last decade. When they reached the shore, he walked up to them and said only, "Hello."

Margaret turned to see who was speaking and then immediately wrapped her arms around his neck. "Oh, how wonderful it is to see you!" she exclaimed.

He gave her a quick kiss as a sign of affection, even though he was not truly sure how this would go.

Then she turned and pointed to the young girl and excitedly said, "This is your daughter!"

Alistar gazed at her; she did not show any emotion.

He could see the likeness to himself. Then he wrapped his arms around her and gave her a big hug and kiss.

Margaret leaned down to her and said, "This is your father, Allie. You finally get to meet him!"

As he stood close to Margaret, he observed the lines in her face, particularly around her eyes, and the pronounced "marionette" age lines that extended from the base of her nose to the corners of her lips on both sides of her face. Those chiseled wrinkles almost looked like a set of parentheses on her face. He knew she must have had a difficult time alone, and he compared the wrinkles to scars of hardship. Overall, she was still attractive, and he realized that he must have put her through a great deal during his absent years. Suddenly, he felt remorse for those years.

"I'll get the luggage," he said, "and I made a reservation at an expensive and charming hotel."

Margaret looked surprised. "Why aren't we staying where you live? I wanted to see your apartment."

"It's an *expensive* hotel: the Hotel Constantine. My place is a small military studio. You'll be more comfortable at the luxurious hotel."

They took a cab over to the hotel. A white-gloved doorman greeted them at the gold-etched-glass revolving doors. He directed a bellhop to load their suitcases on a rolling cart and to take the suitcases in through a separate larger doorway.

The lobby was decorated with gold-brocade chairs, loveseats, and conversation alcoves. Carved rosewood creations with cutout designs were at the top of the all the fine furniture. Large, expensive-looking bronze sculptured lights dotted the lobby. Each floor lamp was a goddess but in a different pose. Alistar and Margaret walked to the heavily carved rosewood lobby desk that filled the width of the large room. Allie trailed quietly behind them.

Alistar checked in to their room. The desk clerk spoke French and referred them to the location of their room. Alistar answered *merci* and took the keys that the desk clerk handed to him.

They took the mirrored elevator up to the top floor and walked down a nicely carpeted hallway to room 56. Alistar unlocked the door and motioned for Margaret and Allie to enter first. Behind them came the bellhop with their luggage. Alistar tipped the man after he carefully placed their luggage inside the room.

The suite had a small marble lobby with artwork on the wall that led into a living room, and then there were two bedrooms off there. The magnificent inlaid parquet floors shined so brightly that they could see their own reflections in them. It was eloquently decorated with fashionable peach-colored brocade drapes that flowed from the ceiling to the floor and framed each double window. Fancy brass-sculptured knobs of cherubs opened and closed the massive windows. Margaret and Allie were impressed by the elegance of the suite.

On the far wall of the living room were French doors that were wider than the rest of the two windows in the room. These glass French doors opened to a four-foot-wide ornate black wrought-iron balcony. They opened the doors and stepped out to view the Arc de Triomphe and the Eiffel Tower in the skyline. All three of them enjoyed the fresh air of the spring day, with the slight scent of blooming fruit trees that scattered the city scene.

After they chose their bedrooms, Alistar took them back out into the hallway, and they took the elevator up to the roof, where there was a magnificent roof terrace, a garden with a cupola, and another massive view of crowded rooftops with little streets winding between them. It appeared as if the streets were branches of a massive tree. The Seine River flowed through the middle of the two banks, and they watched boats leisurely cruising on it. As they enjoyed the exciting view, Alistar ordered French wine for Margaret and him and Perrier water for Allie, along with a plate of lemon tarts, crème brûlée, and cream puffs.

After they finished their refreshments, they returned to their suite.

Margaret twirled around as they stood in the foyer. Then she went into the grand master bedroom. Alistar followed her with her suitcases. As he placed them beside the bed, she put her arms around Alistar in a romantic gesture. "This is where we will stay!"

He gently pulled her arms away and replied, "No, I am sorry, but I will stay at my studio on the base." He grappled with finding another excuse to stay at his place. He felt as if he was a hollow man with negative emotions that controlled all his biological systems. He wasn't sure he could make love to her. As he spoke, he could tell by the look on her face that Margaret was puzzled and unhappy about him not staying there.

"What?" she disapprovingly replied.

He continued to expand his flimsy excuse. "There isn't enough room for all of us to be comfortable. I want this to not only be a wonderful trip for you but also a grand reunion for our family! It is best that we all have our space." He knew he was avoiding them but he had no control over his depression and anxiety. He still housed ghosts as a result of the mine blast so long ago. Even though he had learned to manage the demons within him, they remained very real memories that could trigger anxiety without warning—and this reunion was a possible trigger.

He and Margaret were strangers to each other, even though they had been married over a decade, and this was the first time he'd met his ten-year-old daughter.

The following day Alistar met his family on the rooftop bistro for breakfast. They had a fine assortment of French meats, yogurts, and pastries. He had the day planned for them and wanted to start sightseeing early, before other tourists came out and it became more crowded.

First, they went to the medieval Notre Dame Cathedral. The exterior of the cathedral was a conglomerate of finely etched arched stone and buttresses that seemed to welcome them inside its walls. They chattered about the distinct naturalistic French Gothic exterior, characterized by elongated decorative arches and intricately detailed figures. All were stunned with the magnitude of the colossal height of the arched ceilings as they went into the main church. The distinctive, delicate, colorful stained-glass images came alive as the bright sunlight transformed and evolved them, creating different depictions. The light changed as the sun journeyed in the sky and even passing clouds created shadows that refracted light into different lengths and shades. It was a magnificent contrast of light and colors, as if they were being viewed through a kaleidoscope. They were astounded by the finely sculptured lifelike human forms that adorned the massive cathedral. In an adjoining room, there were display cases, and Alistar pointed out Christ's crown of thorns, which he had worn when he was crucified on the cross.

Sometimes, Alistar felt as if he had thorns within his own body as an aftermath of the mine explosion so long ago. Today, he could feel a migraine headache starting, signaling to him that his anxiety could erupt. To hide his symptom from Margaret and Allie, he cut the day tour short and told them that he had to return to his studio. He said that he was scheduled to work the following day, which was a lie, but he needed to get his emotions under control. He was finding that their presence triggered raging anxiety within him. The psychiatrist had prescribed sedation type medication, and he made an excuse to use the restroom so he could take a pill.

On the second day, Alistar met Margaret and Allie at the rooftop bistro for brunch. He took extra medication, hoping it would keep his anxiety symptoms and a potential attack at bay. He hoped he could make it through the day with his family. Margaret was full of news from back home—how everyone missed him and constantly asked for him. He did miss his home and his loved ones, but he wasn't ready to make the long trip back and reunite with his previous life and everyone.

When Margaret matter-of-factly mentioned that she had raised Allie by herself, Alistar felt a wave of guilt consume his body, and then all the harbored guilt for the lost men started to erupt within him. Now Margaret was adding more guilt for him to cope with. He tried to restrain his pent-up emotions, as tough as it was.

He knew that this trip would come to an end, so he asked the Lord to give him the strength to make it through the next five days that they were here. He did not want Margaret to trespass on his feelings—or him on hers. He quickly changed the subject and discussed their itinerary for the day. First, they would walk down the main boulevard to the Arc de Triomphe. Then, they would go to Rodin's home, the artist famous for sculpting the bronze *The Thinker* statue, or *Le Penseur*, as they called it in France. Alistar particularly liked this work of art as it reminded him to think about his psychological ailments; hopefully, he would find a way to resolve them.

Sometimes, he felt as if his mind was all locked up, and he was alone. Alistar mentioned how the French were planning on making Rodin's home into a museum in the future.

Margaret pointed out the statue called *The Kiss*, with a sultry glance and flutter of her eyelashes toward Alistar. He ignored her exaggerated flirtation.

They next walked to the riverbank of the Seine and took a boat ride. It was a gorgeous day for outside exploring of a magnificent city. Later in the afternoon, after they had worked up an appetite, they stopped to eat at an al fresco café, where Margaret and he consumed a few glasses of local wine. He was enjoying getting to know his wife again and learning about his daughter. The wine obviously made the situation easier for Alistar to absorb and digest.

Soon afterward, they decided to return to the hotel. Allie immediately went to bed and feel asleep—she was exhausted from all the walking and exploring of Paris.

This left Margaret and Alistar in the parlor alone. They both were feeling the effects of the strong French wine that they had consumed at the café. Their minds were saturated with alcohol.

Margaret checked on Allie in the bedroom and then quietly shut her bedroom door. "Allie is totally asleep," she whispered to Alistar.

He was sitting on a peach-colored brocade loveseat, which matched the drapes. She sat down beside him. Slowly, she placed her hands on his head to turn his face, and their lips met in a warm and sensitive kiss. They continued kissing deeper and deeper, reaching emotionally into each other's souls. While their tongues connected in a deep French kiss and oral foreplay, Margaret slid her hands down his shoulders and onto his chest. Soon, they were caressing and massaging each other.

Alistar wanted her and reached his hands on to her shapely breasts through her clothes. She was rubbing his chest, and her French kissing stimulated him. He undid her blouse and grasped inside her bra at her nipples. Then he lifted her bra over the top of her breasts and gave her deep rubbing motions. Meanwhile, his tongue was traveling off her lips and down the side of her neck, right toward her breasts. His neck was bent to allow his tongue to lick her protruding hard nipple. He continued a sensual circular motion along her soft skin. Soon, he reached beyond her open blouse and undid her bra from the back. Passion was erupting between the two of them, and he needed her unfiltered love and affection. He placed his hands under her buttocks as a motion for her to stand. They stood together in a passionate, heaving, heavy-breathing kiss like none other. He totally immersed her in his arms, and in one swift gesture, he lifted her up and cradled her. While he continued to kiss her, he carried her to the bed in the master bedroom. After he gently placed her on the bed, he proceeded to fondle her sensitive organs.

She unzipped her skirt and removed her panties. She was naked. She lay on the bed, ready for him.

He stood up and removed his shirt. Then he unzipped his fly and slid his pants down to his ankles. This exposed his prosthetic leg that was affixed just below his knee with multiple leather straps to keep the prosthesis attached.

Margaret took one look and reeled back in shock. "What is this?" she cried loudly and scornfully. "You never told me about this!"

He hesitated, then frowned and narrowed his eyes. Her hollow tone lingered in the air, as did her overt callousness at his lack of a leg—and for being less of a man in his mind. He withdrew his emotions as he walled himself in. Internally, he knew he was a disabled man in more than one way. He abruptly put his pants back on and buttoned his shirt. It was his own fault that he'd never told her about the injuries he'd suffered. *I should have told her. I should have told her*—he kept repeating this over and over in his head. Almost mechanically, he gathered up his jacket and quickly left the hotel room without a word.

He took the elevator to the lobby and exited the hotel through the revolving door as if he was a robot. Once outside, he turned to the doorman, pointed his index finger up in the air, and said, "Un taxi, s'il vous plaît."

The doorman nodded and called to a waiting taxi in the street lineup. The cab pulled up and took Alistar home to his studio. *I'll feel safe once I'm in my own environment*, he thought, *once I'm alone with my disfigurement*.

Alistar didn't sleep well, as he kept ruminating on everything: the excitement of finally seeing his family, meeting his daughter, sightseeing in a grand city, and learning about each other. He wasn't sure how to handle this delicate situation and Margaret's apparent rejection. He thought so hard that he tossed and turned in his bed as if his pillow was the enemy. It was a humid night, and he set his fan close to his bed to cool himself off. He concentrated on its click, click, click and oscillating cycle. The fan kept repeating like a drum, pounding his brain with the noise of its vibration.

He lay awake, contemplating the situation at hand in the darkness of his small studio. After much debating with himself, he decided that his best choice would be to go back to the hotel tomorrow and continue as if nothing had happened.

Early the next morning, he arrived at the hotel and called Margaret's room. "Would you and Allie please join me for breakfast in the lobby restaurant?" he asked.

"We'll be down in ten minutes," Margaret said in a monotone.

When she arrived, she gave Alistar a brief kiss on his cheek.

He gave her a forced smile, camouflaging his feelings of worthlessness.

Over breakfast, he shared his plans for the day, and Margaret and Allie seemed enthusiastic to start another day of sightseeing.

He took them across town to the Musée Marmottan Monet to view the Claude Monet paintings—flowers, water lilies, and sunrises.

"His Impressionist work is outstanding," Margaret said.

After that, they walked the city and stopped for a quick lunch. Next, they went to Père Lachaise Cemetery, the largest cemetery in Paris, where they strolled past the headstones of famous and not-so-famous people. Many other tourists were there, viewing the stone sculptures on the various individuals' plots. Alistar pointed out the headstone of Frédéric Chopin, whose music connected people across the centuries.

After an enjoyable day—and a lot of walking—they took a taxi back to the hotel. Although Alistar felt they had seemed to connect with each other—a bit, neither he nor Margaret mentioned the mishap from the previous evening.

They spent the following day strolling around the city and taking in the sights. They had a lovely meal at a fine restaurant and then returned to the hotel. Allie was tired and went to bed immediately, so Alistar and Margaret were alone.

He poured a glass of wine for each of them from the bar in the suite. Then he sat down beside her on the loveseat. Neither of them spoke for a moment, but then Margaret said, "I am sorry for my reaction last night."

"OK," he said. He didn't know what else to say, but deep down inside him, her reaction had caused irreparable damage. He swirled the wine in his glass, and as the wine went around and around, he thought, *That's how my mind feels.*

"I want you to make love to me," she said suddenly.

"You know, I'm not sure if I'm ready for that right now," he answered without looking at her. Then he finished his wine, stood up, and left.

The days that followed passed without any mention of sexual intercourse between them. On the day when Margaret and Allie were to return home, Alistar took them to the ship dock, gave each a sweet kiss, and said goodbye.

About six months later, Alistar was discharged from the service, which was traumatic for him. Even though he was returning to his previous life, he felt that he was a different person.

He was able to fly home to Connecticut, although air travel wasn't widely used. Still, it was only a little over a day's trip, compared to sea travel, which could take a few days.

Margaret and Allie, along with Alistar's mother and brother, met him at the airport. They exchanged lots of joyous hugs and kisses. It was a true reuniting of the family.

Margaret was still living in her family's large house. She and Alistar never bought a house of their own. Everything had been put on a long and unforeseen hold when he went overseas.

They returned to her family's house, where a small welcome-home party was ready for him. His mother-in-law, Rachael, talked constantly, and that irritated Alistar at times. When the evening ended, Margaret and he retired to their bedroom.

Alistar felt awkward, but he undressed in front of Margaret. Then he sat on the edge of the bed to remove his wooden leg. He undid the leather straps that wrapped around his limb and undid the netting and the suction cup that held the limb to his body.

Margaret remained silent but watched intently. Then she took off her dress and stood in front of him in her slip. She slid the slip over her head, revealing her bra and panties.

Alistar lay back in the bed and pulled the sheet over himself. He turned on his side, away from Margaret.

When she saw that he had turned away from her, she walked over to his side of the bed. He opened his eyes and carefully watched her in total silence. She removed her bra and panties, exposing her naked body to him.

It was as if time had stopped. Neither one knew which one was going to take the lead.

Margaret sat on the side of the bed and leaned over to kiss him. Alistar responded, and they felt magnetized into a kissing lovers' knot. The kiss became more passionate as she ran her hand under the sheet, down his strong hairy chest, past his tightly toned stomach muscles, and into his crotch, where she reached for his penis. Slowly and gently, she ran her hand up and down his shaft until she had it at full attention and fully engaged.

In the same moment, he raised his upper body so that he could massage and kiss her breasts. He experienced a mesmerizing motion of precise rhythm that resulted in a tingling sensation as his blood flowed like an eruption within. The resulting intensity occurred in his penis and scrotum. His forehead and chest were drenched with perspiration. The moment became more intense as he continued, kissing her neck. The avalanche of adrenaline escalated as he put his hand on her erogenous zone and brought her to an even higher level. It felt good to feel her damp, warm crevices and the erotic anatomy of her now-wet vagina. Then he fingered his way further into her vagina. They were mutually entwined and fueled by each other!

Margaret whispered in his ear, "I am your wife, and no matter what has happened, I love you!"

They were lost in each other in the heat of the moment, and their passion!

Alistar was unable to get on top of her, as he couldn't balance himself without his prosthetic leg. He positioned himself on the middle of the bed so he would have more leverage for his strong muscles to lift her on top of him. He inserted himself inside her vagina and gently lifted her up and down in a wave of multiple pleasurable strokes.

Soon, they were absorbed in the pleasure of their bodies as they synchronized themselves, back and forth, faster and faster, until heightened ecstasy occurred. Their breathing became rapid, and they couldn't contain their lovemaking moans as their bodies reacted to each other's intensity. They experienced total immersion and coital alignment. Soon, he escalated to a climax of ejaculation; he had reached a milestone! He looked at Margaret, and she, too, was in a post-orgasm state.

The next morning, when Alistar went downstairs for breakfast, Margaret and her parents were sitting at the table, and he announced, "Margaret, I want us to get our own house." He assumed that everyone had heard their triumphant lovemaking noise the previous night. They needed their own place for that reason alone, but there was another reason: they needed to progress as a family unit. He needed to get back into society's mainstream and assert himself as the head of his household. Simply, he needed to be a man again.

Margaret was thrilled and jumped off her chair to hug him. "Yes, great idea!"

"It's the right thing to do for our family," he said to her.

Despite his disability, he felt she had accepted him as a human being and as her husband.

Allie came down shortly thereafter, and Margaret said, "Guess what, dear? We are going to get our own home. Isn't that wonderful?"

"Oh no!" Allie wailed. "What about my friends? I don't want to move!"

"We can find a house nearby so you can stay in the same school district," Margaret said. "You'll still have the same friends." Then she seemed to think a moment and sighed heavily. "On second thought, I will miss my mother."

Later, after Allie had left for school, Margaret and Alistar went back to their bedroom and continued the conversation.

"We need to go out on our own," Alistar said. Then, without thinking, he sniped, "How could you miss your mother so much when she is constantly talking—a real yacker! She yacks so much that, I'd name her Mrs. Yackowits!"

"How can you say that about my mother?" Margaret shouted. "You ungrateful jerk! My family took care of your daughter and me for ten years!" She walked out of the bedroom, slamming the door behind her.

*I shouldn't have said that,* Alistar thought. *I didn't think how she would respond.*

Later, he tried to talk to Margaret, but she rebuffed him. He decided to visit his family.

His mother was ever so glad to see him! She gave him hugs and kisses then said, "I'm so proud of you and your service to the country."

Alistar then told her about the amputation.

"I know," she said. "It must have been hard to go through the explosion of your ship. I know there were many casualties, and you had a long rehabilitation. You are still my son and not any less of a man. I love you dearly."

He leaned over her chair and gave her a big, heartfelt kiss.

"Now you have to work things out with Margaret," his mother said, "and you hardly know your beautiful daughter. You and Margaret need to finish raising Allie. Don't forget that it was hard on Margaret when you were away so long."

"I want us to buy our own house and set up as a family, but now Margaret is mad at me."

"Why is that?"

"Well, Rachael talks constantly, and I called her a "yacker." Margaret got really angry. Then I made it worse by calling her mother, "Mrs. Yackowits.""

His mother laughed. "Well, she does talk a lot. No doubt about that. Guess that's one of the symptoms of getting old. I'm sure Margaret loves you and will get over it. She has waited a long time for you to return. Don't forget that she had a baby on her own. Then she had to care and raise her without you. It's no easy job raising a child. She needs you to be with her, physically and mentally."

"Thank you, Mom. You are always so levelheaded and wise."

"I had you, right? Think of life as a pageant—you are always in a lineup so use integrity as a solution. The best part of my life was having my children."

When Alistar got up to leave, his mother noticed he walked a bit stiffly and with a slight sway to the left, but she kept her observation to herself.

Alistar returned to Margaret's house to find her napping in their bedroom. He took off his jacket, hung it in the closet, and lay down beside her. He wasn't sure if she was awake, but he said, "Sorry about what I said about your mother. It was stupid and callous of me to make that remark. She has been wonderful, like your father, to take care of things in my absence. I owe them a lot."

Margaret hesitated for a moment then said, "That's fine. I accept your apology."

They went house-hunting over the next few weeks and eventually found a lovely small colonial house about half a mile away from the Peters family's grand colonial. Allie would stay in the same school, so everyone was happy.

Over the next three months, they grew as a family. Alistar and Margaret grew closer as man and wife. He officially retired from military service and found a job as an accountant in downtown Mystic.

One day he received an alarming phone call. The

caller said, "Come to the hospital right away! Your wife and daughter were involved in a car accident!"

He flew out the door and went to the hospital. In the emergency room, a doctor approached him and solemnly said, "Your wife is in critical condition. I am so sorry, but Allie has died." Immediately, the doctor led Alistar to an examination room, where Margaret was on a gurney, covered with blood. The nurses were running intravenous fluids into her arms. An oxygen mask was on her face, and electrodes were attached to her chest.

Alistar leaned close to her face as she whispered, "I have … loved … you." She clearly was having severe difficulty breathing. Then she took one last gasp of air; her eyes rolled to the top of her head, and she passed. Her body was still.

Alistar held her hand, his head still close to her cheek, and wildly sobbed. The nurses had to assist him out the door. The doctor took Alistar to a private waiting room and helped him to sit on a small couch. He then went to a back counter, where there was a pot of hot coffee, and he poured a cup for Alistar.

As he handed the cup to Alistar, he said compassionately, "I am so sorry for your loss. I understand how devastating this is. We did everything we could to save them, but their injuries were too severe. They both had internal bleeding with multiple fractures." He placed his hand on Alistar's shoulder. "There is grief counseling available, if you need some help."

Alistar wiped the tears from his face. In a shaky voice,

he asked, "What happened? How did this happen? Who did this? What do you know?"

"It was reported that a garbage truck ran a stop sign as Margaret and Allie were crossing the street. The truck just … ran into them."

"I can't understand. Who would do such a thing?"

"The police are investigating, but they believe that the driver was drunk."

Alistar's eyebrows furrowed in anger and disbelief. He quickly left the hospital, only to feel weak and unsteady. Tears blinded his vision, and he was experiencing erratic breathing. It felt like a tight clamp was on his chest! His prosthetic leg felt like it was going to collapse and fall off his body. He felt weak, as if gravity was pulling him down. He lowered himself to the curb at the ambulance entrance, only to vomit his stomach contents as his whole body reacted to grief and shock.

He couldn't believe the injustice. *How could I lose the people who meant the most to me?* He continued to sit and sob uncontrollably, until his mother and brother came to get him.

The preparation, the wake, and the funeral almost killed Alistar. He felt that he was in a nightmare. Not only was he in disbelief, but it triggered his anxiety and depression that had started when the mine detonated, blew his ship apart, and took his leg. He couldn't bring himself to go back to work. It was as if another bomb had gone off in his life. He would sit in the living room of their house and wait for Margaret and Allie to come home to him. He would imagine them coming in and telling him about their experiences, as they had done when they were alive. That had been so joyful for him! They finally had been getting to know each other and functioning as a true family.

Alistar's mother dropped by each day to check on him. Others came by with food to help him cope with his great loss. Finally, his mother contacted his old navy buddy Tom, from Texas. Soon, Tom flew up to visit Alistar.

Alistar's mother took Tom to the house, where Alistar had been sitting for countless hours in deep grief and depression. Alistar was surprised to see his old buddy. They shook hands, and then Tom leaned over and embraced Alistar in a comforting hug.

Over the next few hours, they talked and caught up on everything. It seemed to distract Alistar from his grief.

"At one point," Alistar told Tom, "I was lost within the confines of my past and memories. I thought I was losing my mind."

"You've been dealt a difficult hand," Tom said. "You should be honest with yourself so you can bring closure to Margaret and Allie's untimely, tragic deaths."

Alistar shrugged. "How do I do that?"

"First, move out of this house," Tom suggested. "You have memories here that seem to haunt you. Next, engage an attorney to sue for your wife's and daughter's wrongful deaths. It won't bring them back, but it could help with closure." Tom shifted in his seat to look Alistar directly in his eyes. "Look, you were a victim on an unfortunate voyage. Please end this doom and gloom!" Then, as if it was a passing thought, he blurted out, "Why not visit that Ava? Remember? She supposedly had a baby by you, way back when. It might be an old carcass of a past love affair, but give it a try."

Alistar had totally forgotten about Ava, and Tom had to jar his memory to the time they were docked in Boston. They both laughed, which was a change of atmosphere for the solemn situation that had reunited them. They joked, as men do, about getting into a girl's pants and "scoring a lucky fuck." They reminisced about being young men on the prowl for sex—feel-good, recreational sex that resulted in a boost of self-esteem.

"We could have obtained an Olympic medal if sex had been a sport," Tom said, and they both laughed. "Hell, the Great War had just ended, and we had to kill or be killed in a world plagued by a pandemic that could have killed us. We deserved an easy fuck for everything that we did!"

After all the laughter, Alistar did wonder what had happened to that woman in Boston, Ava, and if she actually had his baby. *If so, was it a boy or a girl?*

Tom left Alistar after two weeks of what he called "friendship therapy," saying, "I hope I've directed you on a path to end your gloom and doom."

Alistar nodded. "I'm thankful for your help."

Alistar eventually sold the house and successfully sued the drunk driver who had killed his wife and daughter. It was minimal satisfaction, as Alistar still missed them so much. It seemed that just when he had learned to cope with his physical limitations and his revolving-door psychological issues that he had become happy with his family. Now they were gone, leaving him with more depression and a rebound of psychological issues. It was another blow for him.

His life was mundane now, but he found some comfort in it. He became a workaholic accountant, which helped to disguise his pain and provide therapy, in a sense. Occasionally, though not often, he would think about that woman back in Boston.

# CHAPTER EIGHT

## Ava Again

One of Alistar's clients was a private investigator so because he knew the man, he decided to hire him to obtain information on Ava. He didn't remember much about her, other than that she was beautiful with an incredible figure. If he hadn't been engaged to Margaret at the time, he might have stayed around Jamaica Plain for Ava. Sometimes he fantasized about the incredible sex they had experienced together. Her body intertwined with his was like no other woman, including Margaret. *Maybe I should renew my acquaintance with her and see what happened to her*, he thought. *Tom did say she* supposedly *was pregnant by me. If so, that means I have another child somewhere in the world!* That thought was good for his male ego. It also gave him a goal to pursue this issue.

"I'm afraid I don't remember her last name," Alistar told the investigator.

"It will be difficult to find a woman named Ava but

not impossible," the investigator said. "Not knowing her last name does make things harder, though. I can go to Jamaica Plain and search all the birth records of a woman with the first name of Ava who gave birth nine months after you docked in Boston. It will be very time-consuming and expensive, as I'll need to do all the research by hand. Then, there's a chance that she's moved away, and I won't be able to locate her at all."

"Yes, I know it can be expensive and may yield few or no results," Alistar said, "but I think it's worthwhile to at least try."

It was nearly eight months later that the investigator called to see him. Alistar experienced an unexpected avalanche of impatience as he was about to learn what had happened to that woman named Ava.

The investigator and Alistar agreed to meet at a small diner near the Mystic Seaport Museum. Alistar enjoyed watching the ships majestically roll in and out of the harbor; it reminded him of when he was in the navy. As he waited, he realized that the mine blast was a faded memory; he had learned to cope with it. He would never forget it, but that awful memory was stored in the back of his mind. Progress had been made. Occasionally, he did suffer migraines, often set off by stress. And sometimes, he experienced night terrors that left him drenched in sweat. They were not just bad dreams but vivid nightmares. *Some things just never leave a person*, he thought. *They only fade a bit.*

The investigator came in and joined Alistar at a table. "Hello, hope you have been well," the man said.

Alistar had been in such deep thought that he was startled when the man spoke. He quickly came to his senses. "Yes, and you?"

"Good, good," the man replied. He reached into a large manila envelope and removed a pile of papers. Then he neatly lined them up on the table.

A cute Asian waitress came over to the table. "Ready to order?" she asked, interrupting their conversation.

"Coffee," the man said abruptly.

"Just coffee for me, too," Alistar said. He was getting anxious and excited to learn what the investigator had discovered.

"Well. Your old girlfriend has been very busy," the investigator said after the waitress walked away. "It took many hours to locate her, but the fact is, she did indeed have a baby roughly nine months after you were in port. Looks like she lived at her family's house and her last name was Daly. She stayed there about three months, and then she moved to an apartment in Jamaica Plain. Seems she went back with her family, but they had another address. I am assuming the family moved frequently because they couldn't afford the rent. Through the years, the family had quite a few addresses. Interestingly enough, I found a passport on her with her last name of Daly, and she had gone to Italy. She traveled with a Devon McDougal, who was a well-known builder in Brookline at the time. He has since died. Then she had another baby, a girl. Devon McDougal was listed as the father on the birth certificate. One thing I couldn't quite figure out was that this Devon McDougal was married at the time; I found his divorce decree from a few years later. He was married to a Jane McDougal, and they had two children. Looks like there was a long divorce/custody battle between them. Speculation could be that Ava became pregnant and broke up their marriage. Devon and she must have had an affair."

The waitress came back with their coffee, and the investigator took a loud gulp of his. He set his cup on the table and then said, "Now things get stranger from this point, as about three years later, Ava married a fellow named Scott Callott from England. Seems this man was a great deal older than Ava. When I checked Scott's background, he was still married in England and had a few children there. He and Ava lived at 39 Prospect Street for about a year and had a baby together. Then they moved. Shortly after the move, Scott adopted Ava's first two children. I assume that would be the child by Devon … and the one by you."

Alistar couldn't believe what he was hearing. She must have been pregnant by him, as the timing was right. Then all that with some guy named Devon. *An affair? She broke up his marriage? That's quite the story.* He did remember that she had a knockout body and was very attractive so she probably had a lot of guys chasing her. *She kept my baby, if the second guy from England adopted the two children she previously had.* Then as Alistar was digesting all of this, he interrupted the investigator and asked, "What was the sex of the first baby?"

"It was a boy, born in 1920. So he would be about seventeen now. His name is Trevor," the investigator said as he continued to rustle through all the paperwork he had accumulated.

"So is Ava still with this Scott?" Alistar asked. His mouth suddenly was so dry that he could barely swallow.

"Well, she hasn't lived the average life," the man replied.

"What do you mean?"

"They had a total of five children together."

"Wow!"

"Looks like they were rather poor—with all those kids, of course. They changed apartments a few times over the years, and he recently passed. Now she's living in a modest house in Roslindale; looks like she owns it. She works full time at Raytheum. As I said, she's been busy." He sat back in his seat and started gathering the papers together.

"Funny how she owns her own home now," Alistar said.

"Yes, I don't know where she got the money, but there is no mortgage on her house. I checked the deed at the Registry of Deeds in Suffolk County. Odd how it happened after her husband, Scott, died. She must work full time now too. By the way, Scott's death certificate listed him as an invalid. He had a stroke about four years prior to his death. Some information indicated he was wheelchair-bound. Looks like they cared for him at home so that must have been tough. I don't know of any other men currently in her life." The investigator looked at

Alistar with raised eyebrows. "Looks like you're the only one who is still alive."

"It sounds like Ava was a little on the fast side," Alistar mused. Still, if the boy was his child, he felt like a heel for not helping her out. He wrestled with the fact that he couldn't have done much when he was sent overseas postwar, and then the ship blew up, leaving him in a year-long coma with many obstacles for recovery. He was still plagued by migraines from his past trauma. Now, this news was making him a little anxious. He sat across from the investigator, feeling daunted. He felt an overwhelming shiver up and down his spine and then a spasm in his muscles, signaling an oncoming anxiety attack.

He took some deep breaths, and he sat still, as if he was frozen to the seat, in attempt to ward off the escalating anxiety. He tried to keep a stable demeanor now, but all this information was upsetting. Finally, he said, "It sounds like she has had a rough life—raising all those children, invalid husband, and having to work. Women are meant to stay home and care for the children, especially seven of them!"

"Yes," agreed the investigator. "She never graduated from high school, so I assume she has a menial job at Raytheum. They make radio vacuum tubes, as you might be aware."

"Oh yes. Of course, they're the leading manufacturer of them. Listening to the radio is America's favorite pastime." *How strange that Ava might have had something to do with the production of the radio I own*, he thought. He had to admire her continued fortitude and that she seemed to have managed some difficult challenges in her life. *She raised our son and didn't give him up for adoption. It must have been so difficult for her to be alone and unwed.*

Was the boy really his son? Had she been with anyone else? He'd thought she was pure at the time; he believed she was a virgin. She hadn't even known how to kiss, never mind how tight her vagina was for him to enter.

The investigator handed the stack of documents to Alistar. "You can keep these. Anything else?"

Alistar shook his head. "No."

The investigator stood to leave. "Let me know if you have any further questions."

Alistar sat spellbound at the table for a full twenty minutes, trying to sort out and absorb the information.

It took Alistar time to comprehend Ava's life and past. He was still haunted by migraines, and sometimes, just thinking of her situation would bring one on. Sometimes, he felt like he was slipping into a deep, dark abyss. He was plagued by thoughts, like the never-ending ocean tide, ebbing and flowing. He was a different man now than he was back then. He again was haunted by images of the ship's blast, which would bring back horrifying imagery right before his eyes. He had to be cautious with renewing his relationship with the past—and Ava. He definitely had to be cautious for himself, but the thought that he had a living son gave him the motivation to continue.

After contemplating his next move for months, he convinced himself to go to Boston and track down Ava.

He booked a hotel on Huntington Avenue. That way, he could have time to discreetly stake out her house—and her. He could play amateur investigator himself. He was dying to see her and to see what she looked like. The fact that she'd had seven babies made Alistar think she was probably overweight with faded beauty. *Heck, women change drastically from when they are young and beautiful. Women are like flowers—quick to bloom and fast to decay.*

It was a two-hour drive to Boston, and he had plenty of time to think. He told himself that he didn't expect much. Ava had faced many obstacles so she probably wasn't attractive anymore. Next, he assessed himself— his hair was thinning with a small bald spot on the back of his head. His face had wrinkles, and his gums were receding, making his teeth look distorted. Sometimes his hearing wasn't as sharp as it had been, and he was prone to anxiety and migraines. His worse attribute was his prosthetic leg. Margaret had been shocked when she'd first seen it. Even being a man now and having intercourse was questionable—he hadn't been with anyone since Margaret's death. All in all, he very much had his own baggage; he was no prize.

*But what about my son?* he wondered. *How wonderful it would be to have a son—something I've always longed for!*

He found Ava's address on Poplar Street in Roslindale, and he located an inconspicuous place on a side street to park. Then he waited. About eight o'clock that morning, the front door opened, and five young girls with an older girl left the house. They were all very cute; he assumed that they were going to school. About a half hour later, a young man, probably in his late teens, left the house. Alistar perked up to get a good look at him. The boy walked down to the bus stop at the intersection on Hyde Park Avenue. Alistar started the car and circled around the block about ten times to get a closer look at him. *He does resemble me*, Alistar thought. *I was young and handsome when I entered the service. He* must *be my son! I was stupid not to have followed up with Ava.*

Now, he had something real—a true legacy! He drove back to the house and parked across the street again. The undertaking, however, seemed futile, as there was no activity for hours. He became bored, and his muscles were starting to cramp. He tried shifting his weight and position in the car. Finally, the girls returned from school. They filed into the house as if they were lined up in a fire drill. Alistar chuckled. *They're so well-behaved and well-mannered. Ava did a good job, raising all the children. Impressive!*

About a half hour later, a middle-aged, well-dressed woman left the house. She wore a black-felt hat with a large brim that obscured her face. She displayed good posture and a proud walk, and she had large breasts—he remembered that about Ava. She wore a plain gray dress with a flared skirt and a fashionable black patent leather belt at the waist. Alistar thought she was possibly ten pounds overweight, but she still had voluptuous female curves. She indeed was Ava!

She walked down Poplar Street to Hyde Park Avenue, then continued all the way to Forest Hills. Then she went down a back street, where Raytheum was located, and disappeared in the side door. It was two minutes before three o'clock. He assumed she worked the second shift, so she probably finished work at eleven. He was tired and overwhelmed with his surveillance. He decided to return to the hotel to rest. Sitting in his car was cramping his leg, as well as cramping his day. He needed to strategize how he should approach her; she probably wouldn't recognize him.

He fell asleep and didn't wake up until the next morning. He was surprised at himself for sleeping so long, but all the information and following Ava and her family had been stressful for him. He was grateful that he didn't have any migraines or anxiety attacks. Now, he was relatively calm and felt stable. He was finally moving on, even as he was returning to his past.

He went for coffee and breakfast. As he ate, he turned his thoughts to his goals for the day. Unfortunately, it started to rain heavily. It would be difficult to do surveillance on the house, but he decided to head over there anyway. He parked across the street from Ava's house, which gave him a direct view of her front door. He was feeling a little more confident about the situation. He had arrived later in the morning than he had yesterday; he assumed the children and the older boy—his son—had left the house for the day on their usual routines. At two thirty that afternoon, the children walked up the hill in rain gear and went inside. Another heavy rainfall started just as they entered the house.

About twenty minutes later, a cab arrived in front

of the house, and Ava came out and left in the cab. He followed the cab down Poplar Street and left onto Hyde Park Avenue. It went to the backside of Forest Hills Station and down the street where Raytheum was located. He saw her pay her fare and hurry inside the building. She would be there for the next eight hours so he decided to head back to the hotel.

He had to return to his job the following day. He was up early to pack up his belongings and check out. Then he went to a diner for breakfast, where he thought about Ava, her family—and his son. He gazed out the window as he imagined a reunion with them. *I have to contact Ava*, he thought, *but it's been so long. She might not want me to reenter her life, especially after all this time.*

"Would you like more coffee?" the waitress asked, interrupting his deep thoughts.

He shook his head. "No, thanks. Just the bill."

Before driving home, he decided to make one more swing past Ava's house. He positioned himself in his usual spot and shut the car off. He sat there for two hours—everything was quiet at the house—and then headed back to Connecticut.

*I need to decide what to do next*, he thought. *At least I saw Ava … and my son!* At least, he assumed the young man was his son.

Three months later, Alistar decided to go back to Boston. He booked two nights at the same hotel on Huntington Avenue.

After he checked in, he got back in his car and drove past Ava's house. It was two thirty, and he assumed that the children had returned from school. About ten minutes later, Ava left the house, and this time, she was not wearing a hat. She was still attractive—she still had her beautiful eyes, even with a few small age lines around them. Her dark-brown hair had only a few strands of shimmering gray, and it had a glow of magenta in the sunlight. She wore it pulled back in a bun at the back of her head. She wore red lipstick and a little rouge on her cheeks. She had a marvelous figure—very shapely and curvy. She still had a tiny waistline, even after having seven children. *Best of all*, Alistar thought, *she has those large breasts!*

His mind immediately went back to when he had laid her on that bed in the Boston motel so long ago. It was as if he was doing it all over again. He could feel himself getting a slight erection as he sat in the car and watched her. He remembered taking her clothes off and touching her soft skin. He had wanted to fuck her so bad. He had talked her into taking the rest of her clothes off, saying that he would stop if she asked him. Now, he had to admit to himself that he had manipulated her and conquered her for his own pleasure. How immature he had acted. He felt remorse that she had become pregnant by him.

*It must have been hell for her to be pregnant without a husband*, he thought. *Society shuns unwed mothers and thinks they are whores. Somehow, she found her way, even though it must have been very difficult.*

He admired her as she walked proudly down the street in front of him. He followed her route as she headed to work at Raytheum. She looked both ways, checking for vehicles, before stepping off the sidewalks to cross the streets. When they walked together, there weren't even any sidewalks, and automobiles were not common. How the country had grown and flourished since the end of the Great War.

She reached her destination and went in the side door at Raytheum. Alistar decided that he would be outside at eleven that night so he could see how she got home. He went back to his hotel and later found a quaint restaurant, where he had a glass of wine to calm his nerves.

In the corner, he saw a young couple, giving each other hugs and kisses. *I miss having a significant other in my life*, he thought. Although he and Margaret had been married for several years, they weren't together for most of that time. He had lost so much while recuperating from the ship's blast and the resulting personal trauma; it ultimately had robbed him of time. The war had caused such agony and anguish; it had taken so much out of him—and away from him!

He ordered himself a large rare steak and enjoyed every bite of it. As he sat there alone, he thought, *Maybe Ava and I are destined to be together. Heck, a son to go with it!* He could never have imagined such a wonderful gift, and here it was in front of him. All he had to do was reconcile with Ava, but he wasn't sure how that was going to go.

After his meal, he went back to his hotel room and took a nap. His travel alarm clock woke him at ten o'clock; he wanted to be ready to follow Ava's route home when she finished her job. He parked down the street from the factory so that no one would notice him. There was a bright light over the entrance that Ava had used earlier. He had to watch carefully, as about eighty people came out of the door at precisely the same time. It was difficult to distinguish her in the many silhouettes of people in the darkness; they all merged together in a dark shadow. He observed a woman with another woman get into a car with a male driver. He figured that was Ava, as she had the most attractive figure outline in the crowd. The car left, but he decided not to follow it. Instead, he stayed where he was, in case she was still in the factory. No one else came out, so he was quite sure that she got a ride home. He decided to do the same thing the following evening, but he would follow the car—it would be easy to spot, as it was an older black 1926 Pontiac with shiny tire rims. He wouldn't confront Ava after work—it would be late—but he wanted to see if she had another man in her life. He needed to know this before he made contact.

He was getting tired of sitting outside of Ava's house. Sitting for long periods bothered his amputated leg and brought on that phantom pain. Instead, he decided to go to the Museum of Art on Huntington Avenue. He spent the day there, walking around the exhibits. He found a section of artists' works with nude drawings of women. One reminded him of Ava. Little did he know that Ava formerly had modeled and posed nude for the artists at the museum.

That night at ten o'clock, he positioned himself at the factory but farther up the street. He positioned his car so he could watch for her in his rearview mirror. That way, when he saw the vehicle leave with Ava in it, he could follow it easily. At precisely eleven o'clock, the door to the factory opened, and workers spilled out into the darkness. The Pontiac was parked near the door. In a few minutes, both the women got into the car and drove away. Alistar started his engine and followed the car, down Hyde Park Ave and onto Poplar Street. They stopped at Ava's house, and she got out. *Must be a coworker and her husband*, Alistar reasoned. He was quite relieved that the male driver did not seem to be Ava's boyfriend. *She seems unattached*, he thought. *That's good news for me. Now, I only have to figure out a way to connect with her—like a game plan.*

He was awake most of the night, formulating a plan, thinking about scenarios and strategies. *This could be difficult*, he thought. *I assume she probably hates me.*

The situation was very frustrating and, at times, overwhelming for him. He was afraid that the stress could bring on a severe case of constipation, as well as the migraines to which he was predisposed. He had ways of coping, and part of that was limiting his time in Boston to two nights. He would use that as his best guideline.

# CHAPTER NINE

# Alistar Reminisces and Makes Contact

Months later, Alistar planned another direct confrontation with Ava. He had to carefully plan his next encounter, as the first two times were very dramatic, and she had hurled scathing remarks at him.

The first time he'd approached her was when she was trimming bushes in front of her house. He had overcome his paralyzing anxiety to call out to her, but it had been an awful scene. He'd called her name, but she'd said he had no right to be there, that he'd left them to fend for themselves. She had said he "abandoned" them, and her tone was cold and callous. She did refer to *his* son, which was a positive note—that kept echoing in his mind. That alone was exhilarating! The boy was his child! *I have to continue to pursue her—and my son!*

The second time was on her way to work. That time was even worse. He saw and almost felt her inner rage and repugnance toward him, igniting even more anger in her. She described fishing through trash cans for food as they were starving. *It must have been awful to rummage through trash cans for food to eat*, he thought. He was bothered by the image of her trying to survive and going so low. Even though these encounters seemed to be going nowhere, it was the only way he could get her attention. *Negative attention is better than no attention*, he thought. The naked truth, however, was very discouraging, and he became haunted by the incidents, which he played over and over in his head, particularly her unrestrained scathing comments, reminding him of his abandonment.

It took him another three months to mentally recuperate from the first two encounters.

Determined once again and fresh with renewed stamina, he decided to make a third attempt, but he needed to devise a different approach. He analyzed his dilemma and gave it deep concentration. Then, although he faced a mountain of trepidation, he rationally plotted his next move. *I'll confront her on her way to work*, he thought. *It's the only time I can get her alone. It's like I'm fox hunting, and she's my prey.* She had threatened to call the police if he came around again. He had to deal with that possibility.

On his drive to Boston, he was overcome with profuse perspiration and ringing in his ears, while his heart pounded violently. How could he maintain an external show of composure to her? He didn't want to involve the legal system but thought that might be his only option. *I have the right to have visitation with my son.*

He waited outside of her house, then surveyed her every move as she made her way down Poplar Street and crossed the intersection. Carefully, he followed her at a distance and scrutinized her every move, even as he struggled to control his jittery nerves. Then he pulled up alongside her, parked the car, and got out. As he stood in front of her, he felt cold, almost frozen, as if the first snowflakes of a New England winter storm had slid down his neck, causing chills up and down his spine. Somehow, in a strong, masculine tone, he managed to ask, "How are you?"

She had to stop, as he blocked her path. "Go away! Leave us alone!" she screamed at him. She narrowed her eyes until they were slits.

He could almost see the poisonous venom flowing out of them at the sight of him.

"Look, you have every right to be angry with me. I am sorry—if that helps. I want to see Trevor. My ship was blown apart, and I was in a coma for a long time. I returned to the States, and then my wife and daughter were killed in an accident." His words came out in a muddled mess.

She didn't respond.

He tried to regain control of himself and the situation. Next, he blurted out, "If you don't let me meet Trevor, I'll take you to court for visitation rights." He looked directly in her eyes, standing so close to her that he could feel her breath. The scent of her sweet breath tickled his nose as she breathed in deeply and then exhaled.

The moment intensified between them until Ava

exploded. "Seventeen years ago! Oh, excuse me—you told your friend Tom that you couldn't be of any help because you were involved with a rich politician's daughter in Connecticut! How was your life? Mine was miserable, and we barely had anything to eat! You have no idea how difficult things were for us! Just a little support from time to time would have been appreciated. Oh no, not you, who was too busy enjoying life! You *abandoned* us! You need to do some soul-searching, mister! You have a distinct nasty character! Unburdening yourself only leads to burdening someone else, and I am not interested! Memories of hardship are all I have. You are devoid of any kind of feelings. We were prisoners in a world with constant disadvantages—never advantages, like you had! I had to pick through trash cans!"

"I was a prisoner too," he said. "I was in a coma, and I'm still a prisoner of my body—I don't have a leg." Soon, he realized that it was a useless situation. In a flash, he turned like a robot and got back into his car.

Ava knew she had some deep thinking to do. Alistar probably would take her to court. She would have large legal bills, as she would have to hire an attorney. Why was Alistar so adamant about seeing Trevor, especially after all these years? It didn't make sense. In the next second, she realized that his reason was to somehow heal himself. Then she remembered that he'd said he had lost his wife and daughter. *He must be still suffering, emotionally and physically, from that loss. Severe grief is uncontrollable when we lose someone near and dear. Devon is always on my mind.*

She had never told Trevor who his real father was; that was a big obstacle. Trevor had been three when she'd married Scott. He probably had a few memories of the past. Scott had adopted Mary and him—that was Scott's idea. In adopting them, the children's birth certificates would be sealed, and neither Devon nor Alistar would be able to find them.

Ava didn't know how Alistar had found her. Maybe he had traced her maiden name to Scott's last name, Callott. The fact that he'd found her under another name frightened her. She had to think through this dilemma to avoid further problems. Carefully, she plotted and launched a plan of action.

The next day, as Ava walked to work, Alistar again did the same *swooping* around her with his car. Finally, he stopped and got out. "Hello! How are you today?" he asked nicely. He stood directly in front of her, blocking her path.

She had to stop, but she didn't say a word as she maintained a blank stare on her face.

"Did you think about my request?" He felt calmer and under control. He knew if he couldn't make amends with Ava that he, at least, had the right to meet his son.

"Yes, I did," she said. She now had more insight into his motivation, but she decided to pretend that she didn't understand. "Why now, after all this time, are you interested in us?"

"Seriously, I didn't know about him, and I had totally forgotten about you. You were the farthest thing from my mind. A couple of years ago, my wife and daughter were killed in a car accident, and now I have no family. It was tragic for me."

She did feel sorry for him but tried to keep her strong outer shell intact. "So you are looking us up because you have no one now," she sniped. "We are the leftovers that you conveniently forgot about. Only because of your 'tragic' loss have you come looking for us. Nice! You sound like a pompous idiot!"

"Look, Ava, I'm sorry for all the hardships that you had to endure—truly, I am. I wish I could change the past, but I can't. It was difficult for me, too. My ship hit a mine, and most servicemen died because of it. I survived and spent a year in a coma. Then I spent more years in rehabilitation. After ten years, I reunited with my wife and my daughter. Unfortunately, they were both killed in a car accident. I have been living in hell for a long time! Please, I want to know Trevor!" He took a deep breath and then said, "It looks like you have done a fine job raising him."

In a normal tone, she replied, "I'll think about it. I never told him about you so this will be a shock for him. I need time." She immediately stepped around him and continued on her way to work.

"OK, I'll give you some time, but I'll be back!" he called after her.

A triumphant smile spread across his face, as he knew he had made progress. The fact that he would meet his son calmed the agonizing pain and suffering that had overtaken his life. Her body language had conveyed that it was time for him to retreat—at that moment—and he obeyed. It was as if time had stopped revolving around the two of them. They both had a lot to digest in considering their past and future.

Ava blinked away tears as she continued on her way to work. She tried to gain control of her emotions, but she knew she was defeated and would have to address this most difficult situation. Ultimately, she would have to tell Trevor of her youthful mistake and that he was the result of a casual sexual encounter. She wasn't sure what his reaction would be, but he probably would find her past behavior abominable. Then he would figure out that Mary was a second mistake, made with another man. *He'll think I'm a slut*, Ava thought. An emotional death crept over her; she would have to face her sins of the past. She thought of how to tell Trevor, how to confess her innermost secrets to her son. *I know he'll judge me, no matter how I explain it.*

# CHAPTER TEN

# Anxiety

Ava received a letter from Alistar about a month after their last confrontation on the street, asking when she could set up a time for him to meet Trevor. She took a deep breath; now she would have to sit down with Trevor and tell him the truth. *Funny that Trevor and Mary never asked for details about their fathers*, she thought. *They just accepted Scott as their one and only dad. He was a great father to all of my children.*

Scott had loved and disciplined the children as if they *all* were his own. *I don't think he ever divorced his first wife*, she thought idly. *He probably was a bigamist.* She shook her head to clear her thoughts. *Doesn't matter now. But I don't want the younger children to know my secrets about Trevor and Mary.*

Her brothers, Jerry and Tony, came by that weekend to work on the "scuttle-a-day" water heater in Ava's kitchen. It was a large three-foot-tall metal tank that required one scuttle, or bucket, of coal to heat the water in the storage tank. Because she couldn't heat up any water, they cleaned the coal chamber and repaired it to a working condition. When they were finished, Ava thanked them then informed her brothers of her encounters with Alistar.

"That scumbag!" Tony yelled without hesitation.

"Please keep your voice down," Ava said. "The children will hear you."

"So how did this come about?" Jerry asked.

"The first time, I was gardening out in front, and he called my name. I was flabbergasted! Then he followed me to work."

"So he's been following you?" Jerry asked.

"Yes, we had a confrontation, and it wasn't good."

"What happened?" Tony asked.

Ava sighed heavily. "He said he'd been overseas, and his ship exploded. He was injured and took a long time to recuperate. When he finally returned home, his wife and child were killed in an accident."

Jerry pursed his lips in disbelief. "Do you believe him?"

"And now he's seeking you!" Tony added. "That disgusting prick! Tell him to fuck off!"

Jerry narrowed his eyes and asked, "What else does he want?"

"To meet Trevor," Ava answered. "He even threatened to take me to court for visitation rights."

"You've never told Trevor who his real father is, have you?" Jerry said flatly; it was more of a statement than a question.

"I never told him," Ava confirmed.

"He could take you to court," Jerry said, proceeding to clean up his tools. "You need to tell Trevor. Be careful with Alistar. You know, your history with men was not good, but you've worked tirelessly to raise these kids. You were lucky that Devon's mother left you money for this house. Otherwise, you would have been out on the street."

One night, after all the younger children and Mary were asleep, Ava asked Trevor to join her downstairs. They sat at the dining room table, and Ava maintained a facade of calmness, an attempt to smooth the road ahead. "You know that Scott was not your real father," she began.

Trevor nodded. "I remember when you married him."

"Yes, I suppose you do; you were around three years old. Haven't you ever wondered who your real father is?"

"To be honest about it, I did wonder."

"Well, I was about twenty-one, and the war was on. There was the influenza pandemic too. It was tough for young women to meet eligible men. Everyone wants to be happy and find a mate. You will want to find someone to be happy with someday. When the Great War ended, everyone was joyous. My friend Emily and I went to a social club, where we met two sailors who were stationed in Boston. One thing led to another, and one of those sailors and I made love. He took advantage of me and forced himself on me. I had never had intimate relations with a man, and I was stupid. Soon afterward, I found myself pregnant with you. Things were difficult, as I was alone. It is something that I regret—but I do not regret having you!" Her heart ached as she disclosed her dark secrets.

Trevor was silent and showed no emotion.

"I don't want you to have sex outside of marriage," Ava told him. Make sure you love that person first. Do not make my mistake. I am telling you about this now because that man has come back, and he wants to meet you."

"*What?*" Trevor said, clearly shocked. "I can't believe this!"

"Yes, he wasn't around all these years, and frankly, I thought he had forgotten about us. We could have used a little extra money here and there to get by. He was engaged and later married a rich woman in Connecticut. They had a daughter together. He said he was overseas in the navy. His ship accidently hit an underwater mine, and it blasted his ship apart. He said he was in a coma for a year and had a long rehabilitation period. After he returned to the States, his wife and daughter were killed. Now he wants to meet you, as you are probably his only surviving heir."

"So, he's my real father?" Trevor asked.

"Yes, honey. He wants to meet you, and he said he would take me to court to get visitation rights if I don't let him meet you. I'm not sure what he has planned, but I was hoping that you could meet him. It would be nice to meet your real father."

"This is shocking!" Trevor exclaimed. "After all this time and no contact."

"Well, yes, he never tried to get in touch with us. He did say he was overseas. He had a friend in the navy named Tom. Emily, my friend, wrote Tom a letter asking him to pass on that I was pregnant—I had no way to contact your father at the time. Your father apparently told Tom that he couldn't help us out. That was the last I heard of him—until now. I never mentioned him to you because I never thought I would hear from him again."

"So how did this all come about recently?"

"He found me somehow. I was gardening outside, and he approached me. Then he followed me to work one day and then again, recently. That's when he told me he wants to meet you. Just recently, he sent me a letter, reminding me that he still wants to meet you."

"This is all too much for me to take in! I am not sure if I want to meet him," Trevor said.

He abruptly got up from the table, but Ava placed her hand on his arm and whispered, "Keep this to yourself." Watching him walk out of the room, she thought, *I have no idea how that went.*

About three weeks later, as Ava walked to work, she noticed Alistar following her in his car again. He pulled ahead and stopped at the next intersection; then he got out of the vehicle and waited for her to reach him.

"Hello, Ava," he politely greeted her as she approached.

"Hello," she said, but she kept walking.

"Did you tell Trevor about me?" Alistar asked, following after her.

She shot him a disdainful look. "Yes, I did."

"Well, what did he say?"

Ava stopped but didn't answer.

"Look I am not a clairvoyant so tell me," Alistar demanded.

"He was surprised and wanted to know why you never had any contact until now."

Alistar had expected some difficulty and mulled over his thoughts before he finally said, "I want us to meet. I *will* seek the help of the court, if needed."

"You know he is seventeen. I don't know what the cut-off age for visitation is, but I assume if he can sign up for military duty then he may be getting too old for you to seek visitation. He's almost an adult."

"Look, I want to meet him, and my patience is running low. I will take the two of you out to dinner tomorrow evening. If *you* don't want to come, then that's fine. I will be at your house tomorrow at five. Please tell him to be ready." He walked back to his car and drove off.

The following evening, Ava took the night off. Alistar arrived promptly at five. She watched out her window as he approached. Her emotions escalated with each step he took closer to her house.

Inside, the children scrutinized the situation. They called Alistar a "date," which annoyed Ava. Mary did not say a word as she steadfastly observed.

Trevor came up the stairs from his basement room. He was clean-shaven with his hair slicked back and wore a tailored white shirt with a tie and a suit jacket.

Ava had never seen her son look so grown up and handsome.

Then the doorbell rang.

Ava opened the door but didn't invite Alistar in. She simply announced, "Trevor, this is Alistar."

"Hello!" Alistair smiled as he stood outside the door. He looked in awe at his son, who was the image of himself at that age.

She held her hand on the doorknob and gestured for Trevor to go out the door. Alistar was forced to step aside. Then she abruptly closed the door and quickly walked down the sidewalk. Trevor followed behind her, and they walked single file to Alistar's parked automobile. Alistar followed in their shadow.

Alistar opened the front passenger door for Ava. Then he opened the back door for Trevor to sit behind his mother. *What should I say next?* Alistar thought, starting to panic. He opened the driver's door and sat behind the wheel. Eerie silence ensued, but Alistar finally broke the stillness, saying, "We're going to a nice Italian restaurant in Dedham Center. I've made reservations." Then he quickly glanced in the rearview mirror and asked Trevor, "How old are you?"

"Seventeen."

"Do you work?" Alistar asked.

"Yes, at an assembly factory," Trevor politely answered, "and delivering newspapers in the morning. I dropped out of high school to help support the family."

Shortly, they arrived at the restaurant, and the maître d' showed them to their table. Alistar told them to order whatever they wanted. They read their menus in difficult, strained silence. The waiter approached to take their drink orders. Alistar ordered Trevor a soda and a bottle of wine for the table.

When he ordered the wine, Ava thought back to the moonshine he'd had in Boston Common so long ago, and that was her youthful demise. She had gotten drunk, and he'd taken advantage of her. *Will he attempt to sway me again?* she wondered. *No, I'm too smart for that!*

When the waiter returned to take their orders, Alistar ordered shrimp scampi. Ava and Trevor followed his lead and ordered the same thing.

Alistar then asked Trevor, "Do you know who I am?"

Trevor nodded. "My mother said that you are my real father."

"Yes, I met your mother but then was sent overseas to dismantle enemies' naval ships. An underwater mine exploded that blew my ship apart. As a result of incapacitating injuries, I spent a year in a coma and then endured a long road of recuperation and rehabilitation."

Ava sat quietly as Alistar ran the show. He poured wine into her glass, even as she said, "No thank you," and put her hand over the top of the wine glass.

He ignored her clear request and then said, "Raise your glasses so we can toast this reunion!" He looked directly at Ava, then gestured for her to raise her glass. "To us!"

Ava raised her glass and then tapped Trevor's and Alistar's glass. She took a small sip, then put it back on the table.

Most certainly, Alistar was entertaining, and she could see Trevor seemed impressed with Alistar's tales of naval duty. He even said that he would like to join the navy.

A small three-person band began playing at the front of the dining room. Alistar heard a slow song, got up from the table, and stood next to Ava's chair. He politely held out his hand as he asked, "Would you like to dance?"

Ava was unprepared and shook her head 'no'.

Trevor smiled encouragingly. "Go ahead, Mom!"

Alistar's hand was still extended, and Ava slowly put her hand in his and stood up. They proceeded to the dance floor, where he put one hand on her back and held out his other hand for her hand. Their bodies slightly touched, and Alistar pressed his cheek against her cheek, saying, "You know, it's been a long time since I held you this close." He moved his body closer to her body.

*He's not only trying to mend fences*, Ava thought. *He's also trying to make a move on me. He probably thinks that I'm easy!* That angered her.

Suddenly, Trevor's chair tipped over backward, and he was on the floor, gasping for air. Total confusion erupted in the dining room as everyone, including Ava and Alistar, ran back to their table.

Alistar leaned over Trevor, who was gasping for air. His face was swelling and turning blue. "I think he's going into anaphylactic shock!" Alistar told Ava. "Is Trevor allergic to shellfish?" Before she could answer, Alistar told the waiter to call for an ambulance which arrived within minutes.

The emergency medical attendants quickly took Trevor's vital signs and transferred him to a stretcher!

Then they rolled him outside and placed him in the ambulance. The flashing lights went on, and they drove quickly to the hospital.

Simultaneously, Alistar motioned to Ava to gather her belongings, and they got in his car to follow the speeding ambulance to the hospital.

Ava was in a state of shock; she felt helpless, and now she was relying on Alistar!

At the hospital, doctors and nurses crowded around Trevor. Alistar informed the doctor that Trevor had ingested shellfish and that he might be allergic to it. Alistar and Ava were told to sit in the waiting room as the medical team assessed Trevor.

Ava grabbed Alistar's arm in fear; she could hear her son gasping for air. "I don't understand what's happening!" she wailed. She took deep breaths, trying to compose herself.

About forty-five minutes later, a doctor emerged. "Your son is fine," he said. "Trevor had an anaphylactic shock reaction, possibly secondary to his potential allergy to shellfish. He's going to be all right."

Ava felt relieved. *I could use a bottle or two of that wine now*, she thought. Then she turned to Alistar. "Thank you for everything."

"Funny that neither of you, his parents, knew he would have that reaction," the doctor said. "At least now you know that he can't have shellfish."

"My brother has the same allergy," Alistar added.

Trevor was released from the hospital later that night, and Alistar took them home. As he walked them to the door, Trevor was still a little unsteady from the medication and went right inside. Ava and Alistar stood at the door in the dark.

"Look, I know you hate me, and I am sorry for not being there for you and for him," Alistar said quietly. "I wish I could change things, but I can't. Please forgive me." Then he abruptly turned around and walked back to his car.

Ava watched him drive away. All she could hear were the crickets chirping in the night—with her thoughts.

Caroline stopped by the following day. Ava was glad to see her friend. She told her about the previous evening's dinner with Alistar, and her voice broke as she described Trevor's frightening reaction to eating shrimp.

"How devastating that must have been for you!" Caroline exclaimed. "How awful to witness Trevor in such a state." Then she said, "But I'm confused. You never mentioned that you already had a baby when you were in Italy. When did Alistar come into your life?"

Ava assumed that Caroline would see her as promiscuous and easy when she told her about Alistar, and she braced herself for Caroline's reaction. "I knew how the world would judge me, being unwed and with a baby. Alistar took advantage of me. It was the first time I had sex—and I got caught. Devon knew about Trevor and accepted my situation. He had Brendon and was estranged from Jane at the time. We were both unattached."

"That must have been so difficult for you! I give you credit, as you managed to raise such a wonderful son!

The world puts so much emphasis on a woman being a virgin when she gets married. Now, explain how this man Alistar has come back into your life."

"Well, he literally just showed up at my door one day. It has been difficult, dealing with my past and my mistakes. Don't get me wrong; I love all my children. I would never think of giving them up, but it has been hard. Alistar was previously married but his wife and daughter were killed. Now he seems focused on having a relationship with his son, even though he never helped me, and I never heard from him until now."

"Maybe he wants a relationship with you also," Caroline suggested in her Italian accent.

"I doubt that," Ava said. "It's too late for me. I just want to be left alone to raise my children. I have had enough men in my life."

"Yes, and you had Mary by Devon."

*Is she criticizing me?* Ava wondered.

"You have had nearly insurmountable challenges. I can't imagine going through everything you went through—and you were alone! Many years ago, when I was in Spain, I did a pilgrimage on the Camino, the old road to Santiago de Compostela, to enlighten my faith. There are many lessons to learn there, and one is you have to rely on yourself and have faith in yourself to find the inner strength that we all have. I am sure a positive attitude is what carried you through all the rough times and landed you here. You have a lot to be thankful for, and I know you worked very hard. Sometimes, the longest journey is the one from the mind to the heart. That comes before wisdom."

"Gee, Caroline, you have such wisdom yourself! We always got along, and now I'm reminded of why I like you so much. Let me add that the 'journey from the mind to the heart' is what got me into trouble both times—first with Alistar and later with Devon. You see, my mind was delirious and my body was desirous for both men as my heart ached for them."

Two days later, as Ava walked to work, Alistar drove past her, pulled over, and parked his car.

"His repetitious behavior is getting predictable," she muttered.

He got out of the car and waited for her.

She stopped in front of him and stood motionless, wrestling with her thoughts. *What a milestone moment for us, that we both experienced Trevor in a medical emergency. If Alistar hadn't ordered the shrimp scampi, then Trevor probably wouldn't have ordered it, and then he would not have gone into anaphylactic shock.* In a sense, she blamed Alistar. On the other hand, it was good to know about Trevor's allergy to shellfish. *Heck, that could have happened when he was with someone else, and maybe they wouldn't have recognized it or managed the care as quickly. Trevor could have died.* The bottom line was that Alistar had recognized Trevor's reaction and had acted upon it. She was trying to synthesize the situation and her thoughts in a few seconds. *There are advantages and disadvantages to befriending Alistar*, she thought. *I do owe him a thank-you for his quick response.*

"Hi," he said. He stepped closer to her and kept his head slightly bowed.

"Hi," she said.

"Quite a night—at the restaurant," he stated.

"Yes, quite a night. Thank you for your assistance." It killed her to say that, as this was the man who had taken full advantage of her when she was young. He had impregnated her and never looked back in all these years. She'd had such hardship, single-handedly caring for Trevor and herself. Alistar never tried to get in touch with her or offer any assistance. She knew he had the means to help them too. In her heart, she was wildly crying, but she maintained her composure in front of this man—the father of her son. *I must appear grateful.*

The conversation was exhausting. Alistar shifted his stance uncomfortably; then, after a few seconds of silence, he said, "I wanted to see how things were. I assume Trevor is fine now."

Ava was at a loss for words and only nodded her head.

"Great! I must go now." In a flash, a second of time, he got back in his car and drove away.

This left Ava standing alone on the sidewalk, deep in thought about him. Instinctively, she gathered her wits and continued on her way to work.

# CHAPTER ELEVEN

# Getting to Know You

About a month later, there was a knock at her door on a Saturday. The house was chaotic with noise, as the children were running around in circles, as if there was an imaginary carousel in the center of the messy living room.

Ava opened the door to find Alistar, standing with his hat in his hand.

"Hi. I wanted to stop by to see how Trevor was doing and to see you too."

"We are crazy busy right now—the kids are running around."

"Yes, I can see that." He gave her a warm smile.

"OK, come in, if you don't mind the mess," she said. "I'm clean, but cleanliness is not one of my attributes." Then she yelled for Mary to take the kids upstairs to their rooms and get them dressed.

Mary quickly appeared and took the five younger children upstairs.

Ava opened the door wider to let him in and motioned

for him to follow her into the kitchen. The table was covered with breakfast remnants. Ava cleared the leftovers and offered Alistar a cup of coffee.

"Thank you, no. I'm fine," he replied as they sat down. "Look, I know I let you down, and I'm sorry for that. I can't even imagine how difficult things must have been for you. I would like to make amends with you and with Trevor. How can I do that?"

Stunned, Ava stared at him, her mouth agape. Her animosity toward him was starting to crumble. An image of them having intercourse while she was in the heat of his arms flashed through her mind. *Does he want to have sex with me again?* she wondered. Then she dismissed that thought as absurd. Maybe he *was* attempting to make amends. She took a deep breath to fortify herself with courage. *Be extremely cautious with him*, she warned herself. All her bitterness, fear, and anger was starting to bubble to the surface of her emotions. Then she said, "I was a fling to you that you never even cared about, not even knowing you impregnated me. You never cared!" Tears started to flow from her eyes.

"I know I abandoned you and Trevor. I have bitter regret—"

"Bitter regret?" she said, cutting him off. "Hey, just smooth away your cares and anxieties!" Her voice escalated as she spoke, and her emotions got the better of her. "You have a nerve, thinking you can just show up and everything is going to be OK! Like nothing happened! Let me tell you—I had to have sex with my landlord to keep a roof over our heads. I had to pose nude for artists at the museum. I had to put up with sexual harassment on jobs just to keep food in our bellies and a roof over our heads! Yeah, it was that bad! People called me a whore because I didn't have a husband. I disgraced my family! My father would have shot you for what you did to me! All because you wanted to get laid! You should have found a prostitute! You used me! You think I am not angry?"

"I'm sorry, but I am not a clairvoyant. I didn't know how serious things were for you. Tell me about your second 'oops' child," he slung back at her. "Funny how it happened again."

"Look, buster, this is my house. Maybe you should leave!" Ava snarled, practically frothing at the mouth.

"He was married," Alistar said, "the second baby's father?"

"That was a love affair, and he and his wife were estranged at the time. If you want to know the truth, we were truly in love, but he couldn't leave her. She threatened to destroy him and the family business if he divorced her." Ava was gritting her teeth, and her face flushed with crimson in anger.

"Great how your husband Scott was married too. Guess that made him a bigamist," Alistar sarcastically snarled back at her.

"Fuck you, coming into my house and judging me! You abandoned your son and me. I know you were a very nice man with the ideal wife and family. Let's not lose sight of you not taking any responsibility and putting everything in the closet, mister! You are a sinner!"

"I am sorry, but the legacy of humanity is forgiveness," he said.

"What? You want us to forgive you? You are a priest now?" Ava asked, her voice sounding hysterical. "That is what you want? Let me make myself crystal clear. When a person unburdens himself, it only leads to burdening someone else!"

Silence ensued for a long minute. Ava stared at the floor and then said, a second time, "I think you should leave now!"

Alistar stood up from the kitchen chair, its wooden legs scraping and scratching the cheap linoleum as he pushed it back. The sound echoed as it reflected the tenseness between them.

The following day, Alistar rang her doorbell.

Ava glanced outside the window and saw his car. She hesitated to answer the door but he kept ringing and ringing the bell. The kids stood bewildered with puzzled faces as to why she was not answering the door. Finally she decided to answer it, if only to put a stop to the nuisance bell.

Alistar smiled at her as he fingered the edges of his hat. "Hello. I don't want to harbor bad feelings against you. I want to call a truce."

"Ignorance comforts the stupid," Ava said.

Alistar reacted with a crescent-shaped smile, showing his white teeth. The wrinkles around his eyes highlighted his age, but he did look handsome, and she could smell the scent of his aftershave.

The kids were all attentive to their interaction at the door. It was in her best interest not to make a scene. Trevor came in from the kitchen.

When Alistar saw him, he called out, "Would you like to take a ride with me?" He turned to Ava and added, "If that's OK with you. You are invited also. We could take all the kids. I think everyone would fit."

All the children wanted to go and were jumping up and down.

Ava shook her head. She didn't like that idea, but she didn't like the idea of Trevor going alone either. Before she could say anything, Trevor was already heading out the door.

She stepped outside but then held her tongue. *If I call after Trevor, I'll look like an ass, screaming after him to come back.* Knowing she was temporarily defeated, she went back inside the house and the children followed her in. As she closed her front door her anxiety shot sky high as she wondered what they were discussing and even if Alistar would return him. She felt paralyzed with worry!

It was three o'clock in the afternoon when they returned. Trevor opened the front door, and Alistar followed him right into the small living room.

At first Ava was relieved but then irritated that Alistar had come right in.

Trevor greeted her and then went down to his room.

"We had a nice time getting to know each other," Alistar casually announced to Ava as he sat down in one of her living room chairs.

"What did you do?" she questioned as she tried to keep a lid on her emotions.

"We drove around, and we talked. That's all."

Ava was getting angrier by the moment, especially with the answers he was supplying. *Maintain your composure*, she told herself, *or the enemy will know he's gotten the best of you*. She glared at him, even as she crafted a blissful facade.

"That leads me to you," Alistar said with another pleasant smile. "I was wondering if you would join me for dinner tonight?"

It had been his smile that had attracted him to her. Suddenly, an image of her opening her legs for him eighteen years ago flashed in the back of her mind. *I'll need courage to deal with him*, she thought, *as well my feelings for him!* Was this bitter regret or wishful thinking? If she refused, then she would look like a jerk. He'd think that maybe she couldn't deal with him and the situation at hand. He was obviously making friends with Trevor and trying on a fatherly role with him. If she refused his invitation, she might alienate her son. Besides, she was curious to learn more about whatever they had discussed on their drive.

"Yes, of course," she said firmly.

"Great! I will pick you up at six o'clock."

Ava hadn't been on a date since her younger years. After Scott died, a social life just wasn't on her mind. The children kept her extremely busy, as well as working forty hours a week.

She took a bath and then searched for something to wear, but she only had dresses that she wore to work. She did find a scooped-neck black sheath dress. She had a few extra pounds on her body, but when she put that dress on, she told herself, "I look damn good." She did her hair in a French twist with a rhinestone hair comb. Lastly, she applied her foundation, face powder, rouge, eye makeup, and the signature red lipstick that was still so fashionable. She added a few drops of cologne to her wrists and behind her ears. Then she asked herself, "Why am I going to all this trouble for a man who abandoned us?"

Alistar rang her doorbell at six o'clock sharp. The younger children were playing a game of tag in the living room when she answered the door. Alistar looked suave and handsome in a double-breasted dark-brown suit with a tailored white shirt and tie. She could smell that slight scent of a masculine fragrance, as she had before.

He smiled.

She smiled back.

Then he motioned for her to come with him.

She gave her last warnings to the children to behave for Mary, who was cleaning the supper dishes as the kids ran around behind her.

Ava left the madness and walked to Alistar's car, parked at her curb. He politely opened the door for her, and she smoothed the back of her dress before she sat.

Then he closed her door. He walked around the car to his side and got in. "I am so glad you agreed to accompany me tonight," he said softly.

Ava didn't respond.

He put on a radio station that was playing music, and they drove in silence to a restaurant on Huntington Avenue.

There were trolley tracks in the street, and as he drove over them, she could feel the bumpiness of the car responding. *Is that an omen of the type of night I'm going to have?* she wondered.

When they reached the restaurant, he again opened the car door for her, and they went inside the restaurant. He had made a reservation so they had a nice table by a window. The host showed them to their table and politely held the chair for Ava to be seated. Alistar sat himself close to her chair.

Shortly thereafter, a waiter introduced himself and then gave them each a menu. They read the menu in silence. Ava looked up first. She watched the people going by outside, as they provided a minor distraction as well as a form of entertainment.

After a few minutes, Alistar said, "I think I'll have a filet mignon. What did you decide?"

"The same," Ava said. "That sounds very good."

"Good choice."

When the waiter returned, they gave him their order, and Alistar ordered a bottle of wine.

They sat in silence.

Instantly the waiter returned with a bottle of wine and cradled it in the palm of his hand for Alistar to examine it, to approve or disapprove of it. After Alistar approved of the bottle, the waiter produced a corkscrew from under his black apron and effortlessly opened the bottle. He poured a small amount into Alistar's glass. Alistar sniffed the wine, then took a sip and agreed to the taste—and the bottle. The waiter filled both their glasses, then left.

"I remember when this wasn't legal," Ava said, "and you gave me moonshine on the Boston Common."

"Yes. Next you are going to tell me how I took advantage of you from there." He reached for her hand. "You are beautiful! You were beautiful then, and you still are now."

"You are a pathological and chronic jerk," she whispered, pulling her hand away, as she knew that would cause a negative response from him.

"We were young, Ava. The war was just ending. Yes, I was attracted to you. If I hadn't been already engaged, I would have come back. I know I was an idiot for not helping you and Trevor. I know things were very hard on you. You could have given him up for adoption, but you didn't. I admire you for that. I give you all the credit for raising such a wonderful son and the other children. You have done a wonderful job. I'm sorry about our words the last time, but I had to know a few things."

"What are you talking about?" she asked with a reproachful glance across the table.

"Well, it looked like Mary's father was married. I didn't understand how she came about, so to speak. It seems you have a ... loose past."

"*What?*" she asked, now a little louder. "You are sitting in judgment of me?"

"No. I just wanted to know how you had all these

children by different fathers," he said, casually wiping his mouth with the linen napkin.

"Wow! Well, let me tell you—no one got into my pants unless I loved him!" she said sternly, wringing her hands under the table.

"Does that include me?" he snorted, meeting her gaze directly.

"In my immature heart, I thought you were the one," she admitted while attempting to maintain her emotions. She placed both hands on top of the table in an undetectable demur.

He reached over and put his hand on top of hers. "Abandonment can't be justified, I know. I would like to be a part of Trevor's and your life. I can help with anything you need. I would like Trevor to go to college, and I am willing to pay for it. You are the only family I have now. In some ways, I think it was destiny that brought us back together. Forgive me, Ava," he pleaded.

She was stunned and silent.

"There are a lot of things in my past with my service to this country. I have many mental and physical ailments because of my duty. Don't get me wrong; I enlisted and wanted to protect my country, but I've struggled in the aftermath. We were young, but my conscience bothers me about us. I've said it before—I want to make amends. You have done a wonderful job raising your children. I truly admire you and everything that you have done. You can reject me, but I want to be a part of Trevor's life—and yours, if that's possible. A legacy of humanity is forgiveness. I am asking for yours."

His words hovered around her head, causing billowing turmoil within her. Ava could only respond with a forced smile as she tried to determine whether his words showed sincerity or desperation. She quickly weighed the advantages and disadvantages of forgiving him.

He shifted uncomfortably in his chair and took his hand off hers as he waited for her response. It was a symbolic gesture of allowing her room to ponder and breathe.

She hesitated as she weighed and evaluated a conclusion. "Your obscure view of the past does not change what I had to struggle with. You turned your back on me and your son. Now, you want our forgiveness. It is as if you are trying to rewrite history—almost as if the fact that you returned makes everything OK now. I feel as if you are badgering us for forgiveness. Like you want us to have bright and shiny faces since you returned and when you are around. It is not that easy. Many things have happened." She could feel herself perspiring excessively, as she solemnly spoke expressing her innermost feelings.

"I understand this is not easy for you," he said, as the waiter interrupted them to place their salad plates on the table.

The interruption gave her another moment to think through the situation. All her animosity, bitterness, anxiety, and anger were intensifying and practically oozing out of her pores. Then, with conviction and courage, she said, "I know you think that I was promiscuous, but I felt we had something, and that is why I made love to you, even though it was a one-night stand. I wanted you. I am

135

angry with you! Because I am a Christian, I will forgive you, as Christ was resurrected and forgave those who persecuted him."

"Oh, thank you, Ava! I do want to get to know you and my son! I will keep my distance and do whatever you ask of me. I promise!" He had cleared the stumbling block with her. He met her gaze directly and gave a magical, happy grin.

He wasn't happy that she had compared him to the rising of Christ, as he wasn't particularly a man of faith. *If there was a higher being,* he thought, *then the Lord wouldn't have let my comrades perish on the ship. Heck, I still suffer from anxiety and nightmares in which I hear the voices of men suffering...I grieve daily over the loss of my family.*

He had to learn to deal with his issues—altered body image and his psychological issues that limited him. He was thankful he could function at a job and in society. Everything affected him; he just knew how to hide it and deal with it. This was his cross to bear. He also knew that he *had* seduced Ava and taken advantage of her for his own pleasure. Indeed, he did owe her something for her struggles, as he was the cause of her difficult destiny as an unwed mother.

"I want to be here for you and for Trevor. Whatever you need I will try to provide," he said honestly.

Just then, the waiter brought the main course. Ava smiled at Alistar and started to eat her meal.

"I do have one question though," he said, placing his napkin on his lap.

She swallowed the bite in her mouth and asked, "What is it? This is delicious, by the way."

"How did you come to own that house if you had to run from landlords when you couldn't pay the rent?"

"Back to examining me under a magnifying glass, are you?"

"No, no, not at all. I'm just wondering—and curious."

"Maybe you think I was a prostitute? Is that it?" she asked, shaking her index finger at him defensively.

*I've obviously angered her with my question*, he thought. *Maybe a little flattery ...* He cleared his throat and said, "Trust me, I do not think that, but you certainly have the beauty to break every man's heart."

She gave a little chuckle and then explained, "When Scott became disabled, there was no money, and we had seven children. Scott later succumbed to his illness, and he died. Shortly thereafter I learned that Devon's mother left money in her will for me to purchase a house—it was to take care of Mary, her granddaughter. Then I got a job at Raytheum, but I soon realized that owning a house carried bills too. My check alone didn't cover all our expenses, so I had Mary drop out of school and get a job. I felt bad about that, as she was class president. Mary is younger, but I wanted to keep Trevor in school. He only had a year to go, and I felt a boy needed his education. You cannot imagine how much it costs to run a household of eight people. Ultimately, I had to ask him to drop out too. We needed money."

"Sounds like you sacrificed Mary's future first, and then Trevor's."

"Well, yes, girls don't need an education. I hope she will find a man someday and get married. As far as Trevor, I felt awful, but I had no choice."

"A little biased, aren't you? Are you hoping she'll find a man like you did?"

"Look, we were extremely poor, and I did what I had to do to get by," she said, her irritation becoming clear. "Maybe in your social circle, girls are educated and the boys get to stay in school. For us, it was a choice of eating or not. It was a matter of the older children sacrificing for the benefit of the younger ones. Trevor had thought of enlisting in the service, and I knew if he dropped out of school, that was what he probably would do—he planned on lying about his age on his enlistment form. But I think Trevor realized that we desperately needed him to contribute. So it was a true blessing when Devon's mother left money in her will for me. That's when I bought the house on Poplar Street."

"So let me get this straight … Mary had to drop out of school to help support the family, but it was because of her that you received an inheritance to help support her?"

"Yes, if you want to put it that way."

"Sounds to me like she got the short end of the stick. She is the one sacrificing. She should go back to school. It doesn't seem fair to me."

"Oh, I've asked her if she wants to go back, but she doesn't want to go. The younger kids are in school, and she doesn't want to go back."

"What a shame. She seems bright."

Ava seemed to bristle. "As I said, I did what I had to

do for the benefit of the children and our family. I never had any *help*!"

Alistar didn't want to annoy her further, but he had to ask, "If this Devon was so wealthy, didn't you receive any money from him for Mary's support?"

"Yes, in the beginning. Shortly after I married Scott, he found out about Devon's contributions and made us move so that Devon couldn't find us. He adopted both Trevor and Mary so their birth records would be sealed, so no one could find out who their real fathers were."

Alistar's investigator had told him that Ava's husband had adopted Trevor, Ava's words infuriated him as the reality of it hit him in his heart. He held his tongue, though. If he said anything, Ava would sling some crap at him about not being there. And he only knew about Ava's life because of the professional investigator's information; he did not want to divulge that to her. He also knew it was time to end the conversation—and the evening.

They finished their meal, and he took her home, where he walked her to her door.

"I had a pleasant evening," he said. "I'll be back in Boston in a few weeks."

When Ava visited her mother the following week, she told her about Alistar's return.

"You must be extremely cautious!" her mother said, clearly upset. "And do *not* tell your father!"

# CHAPTER TWELVE

## A New Future

Trevor received a letter from Alistar, informing him that he would be coming up the following weekend. He wrote that he wanted to discuss the possibility of him finishing his high school education and applying to college. Alistar also offered to assist Trevor in exploring his options.

The following Saturday morning, Alistar rang the bell, and Trevor answered the door. Ava was sitting in the living room with a mountain of laundry to fold. She politely said, "hello."

Alistar reciprocated her greeting. Then he and Trevor left, deep in conversation. They didn't return until late that afternoon.

"How are things going?" Ava asked as Trevor and Alistar came in the front door.

"I've decided I don't really want to go to college," Trevor answered. "Instead, I want to join the navy."

Alistar, who was standing behind Trevor, said, "He is bright but doesn't want to go to a regular college to establish himself in a career. Instead, as he said, he wants to go into the service. Possibly we can discuss West Point or the Naval Academy, as they are military colleges. He could graduate and start a military career. Graduating from either one would mean he would have a higher rank when he joins the service. West Point is in New York, and the Naval Academy is in Annapolis, Maryland. He needs time to think about his future. By the way, I was wondering if you would give me the honor of joining me for dinner tonight."

"Ah well, I wasn't planning on going out, but sure, that would be nice." She was curious in which direction Alistar was steering Trevor. This would be a good opportunity to discuss things.

"You can come too, Trevor," Alistar said. "We could fill your mother in on your plans."

"Sure," replied Trevor.

Mary was in the kitchen preparing supper for the rest of the children. Alistar poked his head in there and caught Mary's attention with a pleasant, "hello." Then he asked, "Would you like to join us for dinner too?"

Mary stood in the small galley-style kitchen, spooning food onto plates. At first, she didn't answer him, but then she tilted her head, seeming startled. "Oh, no thank you. I must take care of the children."

"Oh Mary, you can come," Ava said. "Jenna is now old enough to watch the children for a little while." She turned to Alistar and said, "She's thirteen, and this would give her a little experience to be on her own." Then to

Mary, she said, "Go upstairs and put on a nice dress, dear."

Mary told Jenna, "Clean and put away the dishes after dinner. Wrap up any leftover food, and then get the girls ready for bed. You know the bedtime routine is always a major production." Mary went upstairs and returned in an orchid-print dress.

Alistar enthusiastically said, "You look lovely! I guess we are ready!"

They went to a family-style restaurant in Boston, where the hostess seated them at a booth. They ordered cheeseburgers and spaghetti.

Alistar led the topics of conversation. First, he asked everyone how their week had been. After that subject was exhausted, he said, "So, Trevor, what are your thoughts about your future and your education?"

"I've thought things over," Trevor said, "and West Point is my choice. First, though, I'll have to cut back my hours at work to return to high school."

Ava sighed. That would mean less money coming in to the household. She relied on Trevor's and Mary's contributions.

"I'm very pleased to hear that," Alistar said. "I've brought an application with me, as I had a hunch you'd decide on West Point. I'll pick you up tomorrow so we can go to the library to write out the application. It's … a little quieter there."

*Yes, our house is too chaotic*, Ava thought, *but is Alistar filling Trevor's head with foolishness about attending college?*

*He could suffer disappointment if he doesn't attain these high expectations that Alistar is setting up for him.* She expressed her feelings. "It's probably too soon for Trevor to apply to West Point. He still needs to finish high school."

Alistar looked in Trevor's direction. "I can go to the high school and inquire how to accelerate your studies so that you can get your diploma. It is not unheard of to apply a year early to a college."

Ava looked at Trevor; he was ecstatic about these plans. *If I don't support him, everything could backfire on me.* He'd talked previously about joining the military and that meant he wouldn't be home at all. At least this way, he wouldn't be far away. She was also worried because there were rumors of another war starting with a dictator named Adolf Hitler in Germany. She didn't want Trevor on the front lines where he could be killed!

Then she asked, "Where is the financing coming for this?"

Alistar answered, "I will pay for everything."

Ava nodded but she wondered if she could rely on Alistar—he might back out at some point, and Trevor would be devastated! On the other hand, perhaps he genuinely wanted to help his son. *It could be a way of making things up to Trevor,* she thought. *And a boy needs his father's influence, even if that boy is almost eighteen.*

Alistar turned his attention to Mary, asking, "What are your plans for the future?"

Mary was dumbfounded. It took her a few minutes to speak. "Well, I don't have any plans. I have a secure job at a factory. When I come home, I am very busy, taking care of my younger siblings."

"Surely you have some aspirations. You're so young," Alistar commented.

"Well, I had to drop out of high school to help support the family. You know my dad had a stroke and was confined to a wheelchair."

"Yes, I heard that. I also heard you were quite popular and smart, and you were even class president! Now things are a little better, and you can think of your own future." Alistar was quite stunned with her answer and surprised that she had referred to Scott as her *father*. Didn't she know her father was a man named Devon? *Maybe Scott was the only father she knew*, he thought, *or maybe she doesn't know anything*.

"Oh, things are good for me, but thank you for being concerned," she replied.

Ava squirmed in her chair from side to side, obviously uneasy with the conversation.

Alistar thought, *How sad for Mary to give up her aspirations to care for her younger siblings. She's the reason that Ava received the inheritance.* He was disappointed in Ava, as it seemed Mary had made many sacrifices and was almost brainwashed. *She said she's essentially happy, but Ava really has this one under her control!* He then added, "I know that you love and care deeply for your siblings, but one day, they will grow up. Think of what you will do then. I am willing to help you with any future goals you may have."

"Oh, thank you, but that won't be necessary," Mary said firmly.

He was flabbergasted with her reply. He gave a smile but then thought, *This kid has been Ava's childcare assistant almost all her young life. She hasn't known anything else.* Alistar concluded that you must give people the direction they need at certain times in their lives to help them make crucial choices for their futures. Otherwise, if direction is not supplied, the expectations for their futures could be almost fruitless. He felt sorry for her.

The next morning, Alistar picked up Trevor to work on his applications at the library. While they were there, Trevor blatantly asked, "So tell me—was my mother easy, or did you take advantage of her?"

Alistar was shocked by the abrupt question, even though he knew, sooner or later, Trevor might ask this delicate question. "Well, the war was just ending, and the whole country was elated. It was a different time, when young men went to war, thinking they will never return. They want to experience the ultimate intimacy with another human being, and I was no different. Everyone is curious about lovemaking—you hear how wonderful it is. It is wonderful! It is like nothing that you have experienced. Your mother and I met, and we were attracted to each other. We saw each other a few times, and one thing led to another. We wanted to join—to give ourselves and our bodies to each other. We consummated our relationship and feelings for each other at that time. I did feel bad after I heard that your mother was pregnant. Unfortunately, I was involved with another woman."

"So, my mom was a fling for you!" Trevor said in almost one breath.

"I liked your mother!" Alistar said firmly.

"Just because you like someone doesn't mean that you fuck them!"

"That is a strong word, Trevor," Alistar said. He could feel his heart crumbling, and his gut was churning up a revolt, almost to the point of his needing to run to the restroom.

"You took advantage of my mother," Trevor concluded with a sullen frown on his face.

"I have made mistakes, no doubt. If I had not been engaged, I would have gone back for your mother … and you."

"I'm not so sure of that. Just so you know, my father was Scott." Trevor pushed his shoulders back in the chair, showing that he was a force to be reckoned with.

Alistar admitted to himself that he had not been the best father. He had deserted Ava and Margaret, who both were alone, raising *his* children. Service to his country had called him away, but he could have done more and given more to guide his children. He could see now that Trevor viewed him as having questionable intentions. *Trevor knows I wouldn't be here*, Alistar thought, *except for the death of my first family. I'll just have to deal with his questions and scrutiny. I'd feel the same if our roles were reversed.*

"I've made a lot of mistakes," Alistar said humbly

from his heart and soul, "but I'm here now. I want to assist you and your family. Someday, I hope you can view me as your father and forgive me."

They concluded the exhausting task of filling out the applications. On the way back home, both were silent, as their conversation weighed heavily on their minds. When Alistar dropped off Trevor, he invited Ava to dinner. She accepted.

Ava was ready to go when he arrived at six o'clock. She looked ravishing in a scooped-neck leopard-print dress with a rhinestone brooch and matching earrings. Alistar caught a slight feminine scent as she got closer to him—it smelled divine and stimulated and tantalized his senses. He knew that he was penetrating her shell; she looked this fine for his benefit, and he was flattered by her efforts.

They had a marvelous meal, and then he surprised her by taking her to a play—the first time Ava had seen a professional play—and she was delighted. They had a lovely evening together.

Over the next few months, Alistar drove to Boston about once a month to see them. Trevor continued his studies to attain his high school diploma.

That winter was incredibly harsh, with heavy snowfall and severe cold. Alistar sometimes had to skip his visits due to the weather. Everyone worked to survive the challenges of winter in New England.

The following spring, Alistar resumed his visits from Connecticut; he often took the entire family out to dinner. They were getting to know each other and interacting as a family unit. One night, Ava and Alistar went out alone for dinner. Afterward, they went to the Aviator Nightclub, a well-known, high-end night spot. They had a great time, dancing the evening away into the early morning. When they returned to Alistar's car, he displayed his usual chivalry by opening the door for her. He walked around the car, slid into in the driver's seat, and was ready to start the ignition when he asked quietly, "Do you want to go home ... or back to my hotel?"

Ava didn't respond for a few minutes. Her head was floating in an alcohol haze after the drinks she had consumed. *I'm ready for a relationship with him*, she thought. *Heck, he's the father of my son*. "OK," she said.

It was late when they reached the hotel. Ava followed him to his room, and she stepped inside, when a long-ago scene flashed before her eyes—the time when they'd been intimate. *Now it's happening again*, she thought. She hadn't been intimate with anyone for years. Scott had been disabled, and after he died, there just wasn't room in her life for a relationship—not one for which she would open her legs, anyway.

Suddenly, Alistar started kissing her and then he went to her neck. Slowly, he unzipped her dress. As the dress opening widened, she pulled it down off her shoulders, revealing her bra and slip. He quickly undid her bra, exposing her breasts, and caressed and fondled her warm naked skin. He drew her into his arms with a cuddling caress and pushed his hips into her pelvic realm.

She felt his smooth-shaven face and growing erection. Then, he suddenly stopped and leaned away from her. She stood partially naked and was shocked.

He sat down on the edge of the bed and said, "I … I have to tell … tell you something."

"What?" she asked. She could tell by his stammer and nervousness that this was something of importance.

"Remember that I told you that I have some flaws? Well, I do. I don't want us to go on until I tell you something." His tone reflected a hint of desperation.

"What could you possibly want to tell me?" she asked, becoming apprehensive.

"I think I've mentioned that my ship hit an underwater mine, and it exploded. I still see men flying through the air and hear their cries for help and then the silence of death. This all haunts me! I am a prisoner to my mind. I have no control over this." He put his head into his cupped hands to shield his eyes. He seemed to be coming apart at the seams.

She sat down beside him on the bed. "OK, I understand. War is awful."

"What you don't understand is … as much as I want you this very minute, I might not be able to … perform."

Ava shrugged but looked confused. "I don't follow you." She sensed an undercurrent that was about to explode to the surface and spill out of his soul.

Alistar took a deep breath and sighed heavily. "My left leg was blown off. I am not a whole man. There. I said it! It is OK if you don't want to do this with me!" His lips tightened into a thin line.

"You lost a leg?"

"Yes. When Margaret first saw it, she was disgusted by the sight of it!" His face became distorted at the memory.

"Well, I am not Margaret. It doesn't bother me. Let me see it." She gently massaged his upper back in a comforting manner.

Abruptly, he stood up, undid his belt, and quickly pulled down his pants to show her the leg with the prosthetic. Numerous leather straps held it in place. "Here!" he announced his voice becoming high-pitched as he displayed his naked leg. He shifted uncomfortably between his leg and the prosthesis.

Ava imagined the horrors he must have endured during the explosion of his ship. She wanted to hold him in her arms, as if she was comforting a small child. He was struggling as his feelings and emotions poured out of him and allowed her to see the real person he had become. It was almost a total reversal from the time he had taken advantage of her and insisted on intercourse many years before. Now, his heart and soul were totally open and on display for her to examine.

*If I were a vengeful person*, she thought, *I could destroy his psyche with a simple rejection.*

There were advantages and disadvantages to accepting him. They hadn't reached this intimate point because she wanted to try him out or see if she was still attracted to him. *Of course I'm still attracted to him—now as I was then.* He'd never given her enough time to see if they could truly fall in love. He was guilty of abandoning them, causing her to suffer severe hardships. In some strange way, the explosion almost seemed like his punishment from a higher order.

Thinking quickly, she got up from the bed and stood directly in front of him. She took his hands and gently pulled him up in front of her half-naked body. She could feel his warm breath on her as he exhaled. She wrapped her arms around his neck in a comforting hug. This seemed the right thing—the only thing to do—in this intense moment. Next, she bent down and gently stroked his leg to his knee and then farther down to where the suction cup and straps kept the prosthetic attached. The room was silent; neither of them spoke. She gently touched his stump and explored every contour.

Then he said, "Scar tissue has little sensation."

"Are you referring to your physical body or to our relationship?" she asked.

"Both."

"Yes, there are a lot of scars," Ava said, "but I think we can move past them. Fate divided us, but destiny reunited us. Somehow, this story continues." In the next second, fortified with courage, she moved her hand into his underwear and stroked his penis and scrotum to an erection. As quickly as that occurred, she pulled off her panties and half-slip and lay back on the bed with her legs wide open, awaiting him. She hoped and prayed that their stumbling blocks now were dissolved.

He removed his boxers and directly met her gaze. There was a gravitational pull as she awaited him. The ferocity of the moment mesmerized them both as he lay on top of her. Her pale skin turned crimson with passion as they kissed. She flashed back to the last time he had entered her. After all this time, she still felt his allure, and this moment brought her back to her youth. She felt an aura surround the two of them with an imaginary rainbow above.

As he slid his finger into the depths of her body, she could feel his intimate warmth in her smooth ravine and in her soul. She obeyed his physical motions as she lay helpless beneath him with her legs wide open for him to take control of her.

Then he grasped her in a tilted pelvic hold and inserted himself to conquer her deep moist quarry. Instantaneously, an intense, mesmerizing rhythmic action controlled him to use his male tool like a piston, back and forth, causing a tingling sensation inside of her. She could feel delightful lightning and thunder between her legs with every movement that he maneuvered to the ultimate climax!

He seemed to have difficulty maintaining his balance on top of her with his prosthetic leg. It was as if he was using his wooden foot as a fulcrum. He rolled to the side of her, and they lay parallel to each other and lingered in the exhilarating moment! They were consumed in a shared physical and emotional ecstasy; and barely felt conscious. Both were floating in a cloud above their physical beings.

Later, when the intimacy of the shared moment had dissipated and the alcohol that Ava had consumed had worn of, Ava quietly got up. Self-doubt entered her mind. *What on earth was I thinking to allow this man to defile me again? Hasn't he already caused me enough pain? Now*

*I've fallen for his allure again! I'm an impetuous fool!* Her Catholic roots haunted her now; she had fallen for her basic physical desire. *The sex was good, though.*

Alistar opened his eyes and looked at her. Then he sat up. His prosthetic leg was practically off, and he needed to reattach it.

Then she said, "Maybe this was an error of emotions between us."

He looked puzzled. "What are you talking about? We made love, and it was marvelous! Now you describe this as an error? Do you have bitter regret? Well, I don't!"

"You just wanted to do me again—another conquest for you," she said.

"God, no!" he exclaimed. "I love you!"

Ava lowered her head. "Take me home, please."

Ava felt remorse and regret that she needed to shift through. First was her Catholic beliefs, yet she'd had intercourse without the sacrament of marriage. *I did my penance over and over for premarital sex in my youth, but now I'm an adult and have no good reason, other than human desire. Alistar is a pompous asshole, but I allowed myself to fall victim to him again. He probably wants not only Trevor but me too. How convenient for him to have his son back and have me as a fuck on the side.*

Then she thought of Devon and how wonderful they'd been together. If only she had waited a little time and not followed her father's wish for her to marry Scott. Then, maybe Devon and she could have found each other after he discovered that Jane had deceived him. Then she remembered that Devon wanted to take Mary and raise her with Jane. Ava again felt anger at that.

Then there was Scott. When they were first married, Ava had spent most of her time in bed, between breastfeeding and being pregnant. She had suffered from great depression after all the pregnancies. Psychiatrists were starting to research the depression some women suffered after pregnancy, and they labeled the condition *postpartum depression*.

Now her thoughts went back to Alistar—he had returned. Yes, it was because of his circumstances, losing his wife and daughter in an accident, that he was now at her door. If he hadn't lost his family, would he ever have tried to find Trevor or her? She was foolish to sleep with him. It was like a sick image of her in her youth, before she had the children and the complicated responsibility of adulthood. *It was his male ego, wanting to conquer me again*, she thought. *Something he did in his youth and wanted to do again—for his jollies!* She did enjoy his lovemaking, as she had not had sex in a long time. Putting that aside, though, she had made an idiot of herself by allowing him to enter her body. *I hope I don't become pregnant again— not another mistake!*

The emotional air remained stiff and cold between Ava and Alistar. When Alistar visited, Ava would practically ignore him. She did get her menstrual period, and she was glad about that.

On a bright and warm Memorial Day weekend, she took the children to a barbecue at her parents' house. Her entire family joined in the festivities. Ava saw her brothers along the side of the house, smoking cigarettes, and she walked over to them. "Thanks again for repairing the water heater. It's working well."

Jerry exhaled cigarette smoke and asked, "How are things going with Alistar?"

Ava bowed her head without answering.

Jerry seemed to read his sister's mind as he then asked, "Did you sleep with him?"

Ava dropped her head even lower and remained silent.

Jerry's eyes grew wide. "You did! I can't believe you let him get into your pants again!".

Then Tony added, "Didn't you learn your lesson the first time you slept with him? *Be careful*. You had better not let Dad find out about him! He wanted to shoot him for getting you pregnant decades ago. Now you're giving it to him again—and for free at that?"

"You had better be very careful," Jerry agreed, pointing his index finger at her.

# CHAPTER THIRTEEN

# Accomplishments

Alistar attended Trevor's graduation in June at Faneuil Hall in Boston. He drove Ava and her family to the event; the younger girls had to sit on the older children's laps to make room for everyone. When they entered the hall, they saw a large rotunda-style room with peripheral balconies. Detailed, massive, fluted plaster columns came to an apex at the ceiling, with finely sculptured Georgian-style vines embedded at the top. Huge windows allowed in a massive amount of light. Faneuil Hall was built at the beginning of an epic period in American history. The hall had played a role in America's independence after the Revolutionary War. Here, her Trevor was getting his own independence as he was obtaining his diploma. Rows and rows of seats were neatly lined up for the graduates to sit in. Following the graduates' rows were the spectator seats. Ava and her family sat there.

The ceremony commenced, and when Trevor's name was announced, Ava applauded loudly. She was so proud and elated when he crossed the stage in his cap and gown. Tears came to her eyes as she watched Trevor, her first child attain his high school diploma. Alistar immediately stood up and applauded loudly! Ava knew he loved Trevor as much as she did.

Later that evening, Alistar took them out to a fancy restaurant in Boston to celebrate.

After graduation day, they did not hear from Alistar. He missed his usual pattern of coming to Boston every three weeks. Trevor received his acceptance letter from West Point and was ecstatic about that. In July, Trevor was scheduled for an in-person interview there.

That Saturday, the doorbell rang, and there stood Alistar.

Ava opened the door and took a deep breath to compose herself.

"Hi," he said in an energetic and happy tone.

"Hi," she replied. She had put the memories of their sexual intercourse out of her mind, but they were not forgotten. She was thankful she had gotten her period afterward. She never shared her fear of another pregnancy with him. Things were just bland between them now.

"Is Trevor home? I would like to take him to West Point tomorrow. You can come too. I'll bet you would like to see where he will be living for the next four years."

"He isn't home right now. He's mowing a neighbor's lawn," Ava said. Her face showed her concern as she said, "Are you sure this is all set? You're paying for everything? I have no extra money for this."

"Everything is paid for. I told you that I would pay for him to go. It's the least I can do for him … and for you."

"Yes, of course," she answered with a slight chill in her response. "We will be ready in the morning. What time?"

"Best to leave early, as it is over a five-hour drive. So, at seven o'clock sharp? Is that OK?"

Ava nodded. "We'll be ready."

Early the next morning, although everyone was half asleep, they drove to West Point. Ava sat in the back and was quiet the whole time. She listened to the conversation between Alistar and Trevor. *It's a good idea for Trevor to go to college*, she thought. *And Alistar has gotten him into a great college.* Still, she was full of remorse for sleeping with him. Everything in their relationship had changed in a negative way. Trevor did seem to need a male figure in his life. Alistar provided him with good advice and direction, which resulted in Trevor's increased self-confidence, which she appreciated. *Heck, Alistar is his father, and he should do these things for his son.*

They stopped once at a small restaurant along the side of the road. Ava sat in the booth beside Trevor, who continued his conversation with Alistar as Ava listened.

After another hour on the road in Upstate New York, they finally arrived at West Point.

Ava hadn't imagined how immense and grandiose the facility was. It was so picturesque, overlooking the Hudson River. "This is the most beautiful place I've ever seen!" Ava said. "Those gray-and-black granite cathedral buildings towering over the river are stunning. Look—you can see their reflection mirrored on the river. That makes it seem even more colossal!"

Alistar stopped the car on the side of the main road so he could get a better view. He took the opportunity to give Ava and Trevor a little history lesson. "West Point was originally a fort. Then, in 1802, President Thomas Jefferson had it established as the first military school. Since then, it also has become a historic landmark with a museum in progress for military paraphernalia."

They all sat in awe of the view.

Alistar added, "It is mostly designed in a Norman-style architecture."

"Uh-huh," Ava said. She didn't understand what that was but pretended to be interested.

"It seems very big," Trevor said quietly.

Alistar sensed he was overwhelmed. "Only the best and the brightest attend this academy, and you have those qualities!"

The interview process went well, and two weeks later, Alistar, Ava, and Trevor were back at West Point. They found Trevor's dorm room and pitched in to bring his belongings into his room. Soon, his roommate came in with his parents.

Alistar shook the father's hand. "Good to meet you," Alistar said. "We're Trevor's parents."

Ava didn't say anything but thought that Alistar was a bit presumptuous. *Trevor belongs only to me*, she thought, *and now Alistar is forcing me to share him.* She let it go; she had to. *For all the money he's paying for Trevor's college, I can move over a bit and let him in.*

Once Trevor was settled in, Alistar and Ava left. She knew it was going to be long ride home, alone with Alistar. She sat in the front passenger seat, closer to him. They didn't speak for the first hour as he maneuvered his way through the mountains. Daylight was quickly diminishing, and driving on mountain roads would become more difficult.

Finally, they made it to a town and stopped at a restaurant. Ava could hear Alistar's stomach growling like a hungry bear, looking for a meal in the wilderness. The hostess seated them at a table, where they sat in silence as they read the menu and then gave their orders to the waitress.

Alistar finally broke the tenseness, asking, "Are we going to remain silent for the remainder of the long trip back?"

Ava tilted her head and looked directly at him. "No."

"We have some things to discuss. First, I am hopeful for Trevor and his future. I think he will do well there. Rest assured that I will be responsible for the bills and for his transportation back and forth. Don't concern yourself with any of that. I'll pick him up for the Thanksgiving break and bring him home to you. I know you have a lot of other responsibilities with the younger girls. It's the least that I can do. Now ... about what happened one night between us."

*I knew things would shift back to sex*, she thought. *He's probably like most men and wants sex as payment.* "I remember," she said. "You took full advantage of me, as if you wanted to conquer me again. Stupidly, I let it happen."

"You're kidding! You wanted it and seemed to enjoy it too." He looked genuinely puzzled by her remark.

"You are talking from that inflated male ego of yours! Unfortunately, I regret it," she said, bowing her head.

"In my heart, I made love to you. It was wonderful!"

"Anytime that you get fucked it's wonderful," she answered, her anger now escalating.

"Shush, let's not spread our business," he whispered as he held his index finger to his lips.

"I find you repugnant, and you disgust me. It's as if you don't have a conscience! You are an inept human being who makes my insides crawl with disgust," she said in a lower tone.

"I am sorry for that," he said, his voice sorrowful. "I knew that you would not accept me with a peg leg." He looked down at the table to avoid her glare.

"It's not that at all. Your physical being does not bother me. It's the fact that you took advantage of me—again. Look where I ended up before when you took advantage of me."

"What? You think you are pregnant?"

"No," she answered.

"It's OK if you are. I'll be there for you. I thought you were rejecting me for not being a total man. Margaret was disgusted with the wooden leg in the beginning. It took her a while to get used to it. I could have a baby with you—that would be wonderful!"

"You think it is sex on demand. Why don't you get a membership at a brothel? Then you can have sex whenever you want it." Ava excused herself to use the restroom. When she returned to the table, they ate their meal and drove the rest of the way home in silence.

When they arrived at her house, he opened the car door for her and followed her up the pathway to the door. As she put the key in the lock, he placed his hand on her shoulder, and she turned into his arms. He wrapped both arms around her and said, "Everything will be OK—trust me. I will be by tomorrow." He gave her a quick peck on her cheek and left.

Ava was not quite ready to trust Alistar. Keeping up her distrust toward him was a means of guiding her behavior when he came over. *How could he have abandoned us?* she wondered. *He must be a person without a conscience. I was so foolish.*

On the other hand, she felt as if she was given a second chance at life, almost like he could correct his youthful mistake with her. The contrary sides of this situation raged deeply within her.

Alistar arrived at her house, deep in thought about the future and what he should do. There was only one solution. He wasn't afraid of this and knew what he was going to do. He rang the bell as he imagined taking his place as the father of his son. A flash of motion startled him back into reality as Ava opened the door. "Oh, hi," he said.

The girls were playing tag between the kitchen and the living room. Alistar ignored them and their increasing noise. Then he asked Ava, "Why don't we take a walk?"

"That would be nice." She turned toward the stairs and called out to Mary. "Come down and watch the girls, Mary! I'm going out."

They strolled in her neighborhood on that cool fall day. The leaves were piling up so that it looked like a yellow carpet with etchings of jagged edges, as the leaf points did not lie flat. It was a magnificent display of nature's grandeur.

"How pretty the leaves are," Ava said.

"Yes, they are," Alistar agreed. "You know, I think our son, Trevor, will do well at school." He emphasized *our son*.

Ava nodded her head in agreement.

"Look, I know I'm a lousy rat in your eyes, but I am asking for your forgiveness. There is no excuse for leaving you alone and not helping. I guess that I forgot about you. It wasn't until after I lost Margaret and Allie that I thought of seeking you out. In fact, it was because I was so depressed after I lost them that Tom came to visit me and made me think of you. Here I find a beautiful woman who I was—and still am—attracted to. She also has my son. I regret missing his growing up years. He needed a father. I would like to come back into your lives." He stopped, got down on one knee, and took her hand. "Will you marry me?"

Ava was dumbfounded at the sight of him on one

knee. Her words seemed stuck in her throat and would not come out!

"Ava, don't take too long. I'm not steady on one knee," he said. His wooden leg was visibly shaking.

His swaying made Ava laugh; he looked like he was going to topple over and collapse to the side. "Please get up," she said. "I get your point. I don't want you falling over. I am not sure if I could get you up, and I'd need to call for help."

As Alistar stood up, he said. "I am serious!"

Ava smiled but didn't say anything.

"What? I bleed my heart out to you, and you have nothing to say?"

"I will think about it," she answered.

"We already tried each other in bed, and all went well. I will take on the rest of your children too."

"Look, there are other issues. My children, especially the younger girls, will drive anyone crazy. I am not sure where we would live."

"No problem about me helping to raise the younger girls. I could move up here."

"It is not just that. I am not sure that I want to be married again." She couldn't hide her slight grimace. "It is a big decision, and a lot of people will be affected by it. But I'll give it some deep thought. Let's head back now. I have things to do before I go to work."

He left her at her door, saying, "I'll be back in two weeks."

She nodded in solemn acknowledgement.

The following Saturday, there was a knock on her door. Ava opened the door to see a delivery man with a large bouquet of red roses. She accepted them and found the card, which read, "To Ava, love Alistar." She had some serious thinking to do. She would have to weigh the advantages and disadvantages of being married again. *Do I really want to be married again? Do I want to have Alistar that close in my life, especially when he failed me so long ago? What if I have another baby? Alistar said it would be wonderful to have a baby with me, but do I want another baby?*

The next Saturday, Alistar was at her door at ten in the morning. The house was quiet, as Mary had taken all the girls to the library. Alistar followed her to the kitchen, and Ava brewed some fresh coffee.

"How have you been?" he asked as he sat down.

"Good," she answered but was more focused on making the coffee.

"Anything new?"

"No," she answered, almost perturbed.

"Look, we can deal with this. I don't want you upset."

Ava sighed. "Things are just starting to get better for me, now that the kids are getting older. I'm so fertile that it's as if as soon as my husband took his pants off and hung them on the bedpost that I would become pregnant." She grimaced. "We need to discuss a lot of issues."

He leaned over to her chair and put his hand on her back, as if to comfort her. "I have something for you!"

"By the way, the flowers were beautiful," she said.

He reached into the inner pocket of his jacket and brought out a small purple-velvet box. He opened it as he leaned closer to her, displaying a princess-style diamond ring. "Will you marry me?"

Ava's mouth dropped open. She looked at the diamond and then at Alistar. "I'm … I'm astounded!" she said. The magnificent diamond was larger than any Ava had ever seen. All thoughts slipped from her mind, except to say gleefully, "Yes, yes!"

Alistar placed the two-carat diamond ring on her ring finger. It shone brightly as it caught the light in the modest kitchen. "Let this ring shine as a token of my love."

She leaned into his arms, and they embraced. Then they kissed passionately.

She stood up and took his hand to lead him up to her bedroom. They left the aroma of freshly brewed coffee— there were other things on their agenda that were more important!

They both practically ripped off their clothes and got into her bed. He ran his fingers around her opening, then inserted them in a firm manner. He could feel her warm juices. Her secretions were stimulating him. It was a sexual loop. Then he started to go back and forth with them, finger-fucking her, all while he was on top of her and vigorously kissing her. His tantalizing tongue slid down the side of her neck. He rubbed her mountainous breasts and felt every contour and peak. He arched his back to suck on her nipples, pulling them up into his mouth as if he was nibbling on them.

She was getting heated up; everything felt wonderful! She took her hand and felt below to his penis and stroked it even harder.

Quickly, he inserted himself into her desirous waiting body. He pumped her multiple times, and then he had a spontaneous ejaculation. His ejaculation was climactic for both of them.

She could feel his warm, wet secretions rolling out of her and on the inside of her thighs. It felt good! She hadn't had intercourse for such a long time—not any meaningful sex, anyway. This was different, with a lot of passion, as if she was doing it for the first time. They were lying sandwiched together when they heard the front door open and the noise of the girls returning.

"Oh shit!" Alistar said. He jumped off her and attempted to put his pants on, but he had trouble maneuvering his prosthetic leg and fell backward. There was a loud thump as his body hit the floor. Ava gave a little giggle but tried to be quiet. Finally, he was able to reattach his leather straps and get dressed.

Ava threw her clothes on and went downstairs.

The girls were in the kitchen, having a snack. Jenna pointed to the velvet box, still on the table. "What was in that?" she asked.

Ava quickly put her hand behind her back and removed the diamond from her finger. She took the box and placed it in a kitchen cabinet. *This is not the time or place to announce our engagement.* "Just an empty box," she said. When she walked back into the living room, Alistar

167

was sitting, neatly clothed, on the couch. She gave a silly smirk in his direction.

The girls joined them in the living room.

"Look who came to visit us," Ava said.

"Does anyone want to go down by the pond?" Alistar asked.

The five younger girls screamed *yes*, but Mary said, "I have things to do. Thank you anyway."

The girls followed Alistar outside, got into his car, and noisily jumped up and down, like softballs in a carnival batting cage. Ava joined Alistar in the front, and he drove to the pond. The girls jumped out of the car and ran down one of the dirt pathways that led to the water. The ducks on the pond started quacking viciously as the girls approached. When the girls were occupied with chasing the ducks, Alistar softly said to Ava, "That was wonderful!"

"Yeah." She blushed because she had enjoyed him being inside of her. "I don't know how you got your pants on so quickly."

"Making love to you felt like the first time," he said.

"Was I your first?" she asked. "I've wondered about that."

"Yes, you were."

"You knew all the moves. I figured that you had experience before me."

"No, I had looked at books and asked how to do it. You were my first—and delightful at that."

"I guess guys just have a natural instinct for intimate physical sex."

"No, dear, guys just have a natural instinct for intimate physical lovemaking," he corrected her with a smile.

They held hands and were walking around the pond when Alistar said, "Look, we need to discuss some things."

"OK, what's on your mind?"

"I have some problems from the mine blast. It's not just that I lost my leg. Sometimes I have psychological issues as well."

"Like what?"

"I occasionally hear voices in my head."

"What? What do they say?"

"My psychiatrist thinks that even after all this time since the incident, when I become anxious or depressed the voices talk to me," he said quietly.

"What do they say to you?" she asked.

"Sometimes, I hear the men on the ship and their cries as they die. It is not pleasant. Then sometimes, I get depressed about the loss of Margaret and Allie. I have occasional night terrors about the blast. My mind detaches from reality, and it's like an emotional death. I don't want to scare you off, but I want you to be aware of it."

She visibly winced as she questioned him. "How often does this occur?"

"Since things have been going good between us, they don't seem to bother me. Sometimes, I do get down and depressed, though. I don't want to lie to you; you may see me experience these occurrences." Then he was silent as they strolled a few more feet around the pond.

"Thanks for letting me know. My screaming young girls are not going to be a picnic either. They are loud, and they fight frequently. I hope they won't trigger any of your episodes. Going from a solitary environment to our household will be a big change; ours is a noisy and chaotic world. You will need an abundance of patience, and you'll need some way to cope to find an inner peace."

"A bigger place would work better when we live together," he said. "Of course, it would be around here, as I know that the children are best staying in their own environment. We could pool our finances and get a bigger place so there would be more room for everyone. Maybe we could have a nice master bedroom that was off-limits to the kids. What do you think?"

She didn't like the idea of taking her money out of her house and pooling it with his so she only replied, "Let's think about that."

The following week, when Alistar took her out to dinner, he asked, "Are we still getting married?"

"Of course, but we don't have to rush. We can take our time." She smiled, although she felt that things were heading toward a tangled mess.

"I see that you aren't wearing your ring," he observed.

"I wanted to wait to the right moment to tell the family. Maybe we could have a long engagement too. Best to make the announcement when Trevor comes home. It may take a while for the girls to accept you and all the changes that come with this."

"I love you, and I want us to be together as soon as possible!"

"My children lost their father, we moved frequently,

Trevor is away, and I work. My point is that there have been a lot of changes in their lives. I want to take it slow so everyone gets used to the idea."

"I get the feeling that you don't really want to get married."

"No. No, Alistar, that is not true."

"You still can't forgive me for not being there when you had Trevor. It's like you are still punishing me." He called the waiter over and abruptly requested the check.

Ava was shocked at his reaction.

He quickly paid the bill, stood up and said to her, "We are done here! Let's go!"

When they reached her front door, she turned to invite him in, but he was already halfway down her pathway.

The following months followed the same routine. Trevor was at West Point, the younger girls attended school, and Mary worked during the day and took care of the girls in the evening while Ava went to work. Alistar only came to call on them once a month. Sometimes, he and Ava would see each other, but sometimes they missed each other.

# CHAPTER FOURTEEN

## Strained Relations

Alistar was scheduled to pick up Trevor at West Point to bring him home for the Thanksgiving Day weekend. Ava was excited about seeing her son and finding out how he was doing. She and the girls prepared the turkey and pies for the dual festivities of the holiday and the welcoming home of Trevor. It was the first time that any of her children had been away from the family for so long. She also thought about Alistar; she hadn't heard from him lately. When he did come by the house, their relationship seemed strained and distant. She kept his diamond engagement ring in the purple-velvet box in her bureau drawer. She didn't see the point of letting the girls know about their engagement until she was sure herself.

Trevor arrived home at six o'clock on Wednesday evening. Ava ran to him, and they hugged, equally glad to see each other.

"How have you been?" Ava asked.

"Fine," he answered; he was preoccupied with bringing in all his books and luggage.

"Tell me everything about school," Ava said. "Tell me all the details and how you're doing there."

The girls flocked around him, asking lots of questions as they had missed him so much.

Then Alistar came in the door with more of Trevor's belongings. Ava looked up at him, and he smiled at her. She returned his smile.

"Hello and goodbye, everyone! I have to leave," he announced.

"Oh, please stay!" Ava said. "We'll have supper soon. You are welcome to stay this evening and then come for tomorrow's festivities."

He agreed but only stayed until eight o'clock. "Thank you for everything," he said as he got up to leave.

Ava ran behind him as he headed for the front door. "Alistar, please come tomorrow for Thanksgiving dinner. One o'clock," she announced with a smile.

"Sure, I would like that," he answered, even though things were strained between them.

On Thanksgiving Day, he arrived with a large bouquet of yellow roses and a bottle of Merlot wine for Ava.

"Thank you for the gifts," Ava said. "Make yourself at home." She immediately went back into the kitchen to get the turkey out of the oven.

It was a happy occasion, as everyone was in a good mood, and Trevor was home. After the meal, they enjoyed the apple and blueberry pies that Mary and the girls had made.

"Everything was delicious," Alistar said, sitting back in his chair. "Anyone interested in a nice walk around the block to help digest this delicious meal?"

Mary was the first to answer. "I have to clean up the dishes."

The younger girls were excited to go. "Yes, yes, yes!" they chirped.

Trevor echoed his little sisters' sentiments, especially since he enjoyed telling everyone about his experiences at college.

As they strolled around the block, Julia, the youngest, grabbed Alistar's hand and said, "I wish you were my daddy."

He looked down and patted her head sweetly. "Nice of you to say."

Ava smiled at his response.

Trevor kept going on about his studies and tales of his experiences, and his new life. At one point, his sisters ran ahead, and Trevor walked faster to catch up with them.

"Can I have a private word with you?" Alistar asked Ava when they were alone.

"Sure, seems like we have a moment." She pointed to the children jumping and walking in front of them.

"I see that you still are not wearing the ring I gave you, and I was wondering why."

"Well, I was cooking, and I didn't want to get it dirty." She hesitated a moment and then said, "But I'm not sure it's the best decision for us to marry."

"That's what I thought. Why? What has changed?"

"You were angry at the restaurant," Ava said. "I wasn't sure if you still wanted to get married."

"Of course I want to marry you! I was angry that you seemed to have misgivings after you accepted my proposal. I feel you have doubts. Don't get me wrong—I want to marry you anyway. I truly love you, but I feel like I am a warrior, battling for your love!"

"Oh! It has been tough raising these kids. I was essentially alone all the years that Scott was sick and in the wheelchair. Everything was hard on me! I wasn't sure if I wanted another man in my life."

"Well, what is the verdict now? You've had time to think about it." He readied himself for her rejection.

"I decided that we should marry!" she exclaimed.

Immediately, he hugged her and picked her up off her feet, and they twirled in a lover's knot. The kids stopped ahead of them and turned around to see the commotion. They ran back to Ava and Alistar, who announced, "We are going to get married!"

They all jumped for joy!

"Fate divided us, but destiny reunited us!" Alistar said.

When they arrived back at the house, Alistar and Ava announced their plans to Mary, who had just finished cleaning up the kitchen.

"Oh," she said, completely emotionless.

Alistar reached for the bottle of wine that he had brought and proceeded to open it. "Let's toast to our marriage!"

Ava poured soda for the children to perform the toast. Then she went upstairs and brought down the velvet box. In front of everyone, she removed the brilliant diamond engagement ring and placed it on her finger. She said, "Let the brilliance of this diamond be the guiding light to our future—all of us together!"

Later, when Alistar was getting ready to leave, Ava threw her arms around his neck. They embraced and had a long kiss. Then, she softly whispered in his ear, "Are you sure you know what you are getting into—a household of rambunctious children?"

"As long as you are here, everything will be fine!" he said with a smile.

Later that evening, Trevor went downstairs to get something to eat. Mary was putting dishes away in the cabinet.

Trevor said excitedly, "Isn't it wonderful that Mom and Alistar are getting married?"

Mary only said *oh.*

Trevor evaluated her response. "You seem taken aback by the news."

"It only means cleaning up after another household member—more work for me."

Alistar now came up every weekend and visited at the house. He also drove back and forth to West Point to take Trevor between the two locations.

He and Ava had a marvelous courtship. Occasionally, she would stay at his hotel, and they engaged in wonderful sex.

During these rendezvous at his hotel, they would immediately strip their clothes off and engage in sensuous foreplay, which boosted their readiness for each other. Alistar would describe the foreplay as stimulating the "human pheromones" and that they transmitted their ultimate love for each other. Sometimes, he would just give her an enticing look, and she found herself spellbound, making love to him. It was as if her internal organs longed for his penetration, almost like an addiction. Their copulation was the physical consummation of their hearts.

One time, he stood her against the wall, using his wooden leg similar to an architectural leaning post while he inserted his stiff penis into the confines of her vagina. He plunged in and out of her as he held onto her hips to control his pelvic rhythm. Her large breasts vibrated with each of his pelvic thrusts. This enhanced his pleasure, as he watched her climax. He took one hand and felt her breasts, squeezing and licking her nipples. Then he simultaneously pumped her so fast, causing an ejaculation of extremes for them both. Her skin turned almost magenta and was warm to the touch as her head overflowed in ecstasy.

There was no guilt for her; his touch was delightfully appetizing. She had known, way back when, that he was the man for her. It was like a dream come true.

Ava continued to insist on a long courtship so that everyone would get used to the fact that their life as a family was about to change drastically. Soon, they started to search for an appropriate residence that would suit everyone's needs. Ava and Alistar agreed that her house was too small, but Ava always found something wrong with a potential new house. She was having a hard time getting rid of her house, as the money she'd spent on it was to be used for Mary's benefit. Soon, Ava decided that Mary was an adult, and she wouldn't care as long as Ava supplied her with a roof over her head. The proceeds from selling the house could be used to enhance everyone's future; that would benefit not only Mary but the entire family.

Ava did feel guilty, though, as she had never told Mary about the money or who her father was.

# CHAPTER FIFTEEN

## The Fury of Mother Nature

A nor'easter was forecast for the entire East Coast of the United States, extending from Florida to Maine. Everyone was to prepare and to have enough food and water to sustain themselves, as regular life was expected to be crippled.

Trevor was at West Point, and Ava was glad for that, as he was inland, where excessive rain was expected but not hurricane-force winds. Alistar was staying in Connecticut until after the storm. "I'll be hunkering down," he told Ava.

Life shut down, and everyone stayed home. Ava bought extra candles in case the power went out. Using candles reminded her of when she was growing up, and they had no electricity in the home. It was especially difficult at night to use the toilet by candlelight. She laughed when she thought back on using an old outhouse. How awful that was! Now, they had their own bathroom right in the house with running water, but with one bathroom and eight people, it seemed the bathroom was constantly occupied.

Ava was ready when the rain came, and it got heavier as the day progressed. Soon, it was raining so hard that they could barely see outside their windows; it looked like a gray mass. It was very dark, even though it was during daylight hours. They heard the hard, pounding rain on the roof and as it ran off the sides of the house. The strong wind echoed and seemed as if it was a monster trying to break into the house. Ava thought she could feel the house shake a bit.

The girls kept themselves occupied by playing card games and reading.

Then, Ava's cellar started to flood.

After two days, the storm was finally over, but it had hit Mystic Seaport hard, especially in the area where Alistar lived. Ava constantly listened to her radio in the living room for updates. All she could do was wait until she heard from him. She was fraught with worry!

She opened the cellar door and found the water in the basement. It was muddy and murky with an awful odor. She and the girls took turns trying to sweep the water out the cellar door. They had stored many articles down there, and they had to go through each box to see what was salvageable, which was time-consuming.

Cleanup efforts were done in the community as well, like removing trees that had blown down. Many people had excessive property damage. Ava was thankful that they only had a flooded basement. She wanted to go to West Point to get Trevor, as she was terribly worried about him, but she had no way of getting there or even contacting him.

She returned to work that Monday, and the children went back to school. Ava expected to see Alistar on the following weekend, but he never came. The weekend after that, he did not come to see her either, and she became even more worried. By the third week, she told Jerry how worried she was and asked him to take her to Mystic Seaport.

Her brother agreed, but he couldn't take the long drive until the following weekend. That was Christmas week, and Jerry asked Ava, "Do you want me to drive to West Point to get Trevor?"

Trevor ended up taking the bus home from West Point to see if everyone was all right.

"I'm so glad to see you, Trevor," Ava said, "but I haven't heard anything from Alistar."

Another two days went by, and they continuously listened to the radio about cleanup efforts. The radio announcer mentioned that a tornado had touched down around Mystic Seaport. This caused even more worry for them.

Finally, Ava again asked her brother Jerry to take them to Mystic Seaport, as he was the only one who had a car. During the more than two-hour drive there, Ava was filled with fear that something devastating had happened to Alistar. *If I had married him*, she thought, *then he wouldn't have been in Connecticut during the storm. He'd have been with us.* Then she silently reprimanded herself for being so stupid!

Finally, they reached Alistar's address—but the house was completely destroyed—nothing left but a pile of scrap materials. It was like a war zone, with piles of debris everywhere!

Ava burst into tears as she viewed the devastated lot in front of her. "Oh my God!" she cried. "Where is Alistar?" She didn't have an address for any other family members so they decided to go to each local hospital and search for him.

The hospitals were busy, and it was hard to stop someone to ask if they had a patient there by his name. "This is so frustrating!" Ava cried. She tried to control her tears but they kept seeping from her swollen eyes.

Finally, at the fifth hospital, they found him. Unfortunately, he was in a coma.

Ava recollected how Alistar had spoken of the mine blast that had caused him to go into a coma. Both Ava and Trevor cried over the sight of him. She could feel a cold wave of desperation shrouding her inner being.

Later that afternoon, a man came into the room to see Alistar. He introduced himself as David, Alistar's brother.

"I'm Ava Callott, Alistar's fiancée. This is my brother Jerry, and this"—she motioned to Trevor—"is Alistar's and my son, Trevor."

David was immediately taken aback and had a flabbergasted look on his face. He directly confronted her. "Are you saying that my brother, Alistar, is this young man's father?"

Ava answered, "Yes. And we are engaged."

David looked shocked. "I knew that he was going

to the Boston area frequently, but I did not know why. I was unaware that Alistar was engaged—and that he had a son!"

Trevor stood to the side and watched in silence.

Ava was mystified that Alistar hadn't thought enough about her or Trevor to tell his own brother. *I have to let that go for now*, she thought. *I must focus on him getting better—but Alistar will have to explain this when he recovers … if he recovers.*

Ava visited Alistar every other Saturday; that was when Jerry could take her down to Connecticut. Alistar had a gastrostomy tube sutured to his stomach, and the nurses ran a line to feed him. They came in every four hours to give him his tube feeding, which nutritionally sustained him. They also performed personal care and frequently repositioned him to prevent bedsores.

Ava's heart was broken at the sight of him. She could see the outline of his body under the sheet. He lay so still, without movement and barely breathing. He was extremely pale and seemed more fragile each time she saw him. There was an empty spot where his leg would be attached to his body. She could almost feel the pain this man must have endured during his service duty to the country.

Later, she learned that a tornado had touched down in his area, which demolished his house. Reports were that he was found alive in the rubble, and they had to dig him out.

Alistar's situation caused Ava to remember how

difficult it had been to care for Scott when he was wheelchair-bound after his stroke. Her body could almost feel the physical pain she had endured while caring for Scott.

One day Alistar's mother was in his room when Ava came to visit. Ava smiled as she introduced herself, and they embraced each other.

His mother had tears in her eyes as she spoke of Alistar. "His life has been so difficult. First, the war and his injuries; then, the loss of his wife and daughter."

"We were to be married," Ava said. "We have a son together."

His mother nodded. "David informed me that Alistar had a son and was engaged. I am happy about the news. Hopefully, he will come out of this. They say the longer a person is in a coma, the harder it is for them to recover. He was in a coma for a year in France when he was in the service." There was a definite weariness in his mother's voice as she spoke. She never asked for the details of how Alistar and Ava had a son together.

About six months later, Alistar started twitching his hands. He wasn't himself yet but slowly started to regain consciousness. He spoke only in a whisper and often seemed delirious, speaking of silly things; sometimes, he didn't make any sense at all. At first, he called out for Margaret and Allie. He didn't recognize Ava the first time she visited him, and she was heartbroken.

The following Saturday when she arrived, he called her Ava.

"Oh, my darling, you remembered!" she cried excitedly. It was as if the sun was rising on a bright and clear day.

Thereafter, however, he could only answer her in nonsense jargon.

One of the doctors told Ava that Alistar would have to learn to talk and walk all over again. "Furthermore, things could become even more complicated with him having to learn to use his prosthetic leg again; it could be tricky," the doctor said. "The brain and the nerve pathways for gross motor skills need to simultaneously regenerate to coordinate and function appropriately. There have been improvements with prosthetic legs, so we'll try to get him the latest model. The fact remains, though, that since he has such a history of psychological issues, he may seem a little psychotic at times. Again, his brain has another traumatic insult event from which to recuperate. The brain needs to insulate itself to heal, and it almost shuts down to do that."

*It's going to be a difficult road for us*, Ava thought. Then, without warning, she thought, *Maybe a future with this man is not realistic. I don't know if I can take on the role of caretaker for this man—or any man—again. I'll have to think hard about putting myself in that situation once more. I still have my girls to raise too!*

When she returned home from the hospital, she frequently took walks to relax and relieve the tension after seeing Alistar helpless. She continued to wear the marvelous diamond ring that he'd given her, but she was confused, and cloudiness covered her mind, causing conflicting emotions. She would stroll along her street at dusk and sometimes thought of herself as if she was alone in a snow globe that someone could pick up and shake. The blowing snow could cause all sorts of destruction wherever fate decided to let it settle. She found a little consolation in looking at the black tree trunks against the dark sky, with their large branches extending outward, as if they represented the multiple choices that lay in front of her. She knew it would be a difficult road with many stumbling stones ahead.

Alistar finally started to improve. *Should we marry?* she wondered. Still, she kept silent about the issue and thought maybe he had forgotten about their plans. She might end up taking care of him as she had with Scott. *Do I want to put myself in that situation again?*

It took another six months before he was released from the hospital, but slowly, he did recuperate. He got an apartment near the hospital so it would be easy to attend his therapy appointments. They gave him a new leg, and he learned how to balance his weight and walk all over again. He did quite well with the use of the new leg.

Ava continued to visit; she came every Saturday now. She would take the bus there so as not to burden her brother. She was happy to be with Alistar and would take the role of caretaker on the afternoons that they were together.

One afternoon, after he finished his shower, using a shower chair, he asked Ava to dry him. She did as he requested and gently dried his private area. He had an erection, but she wasn't quite sure how to deal with his sudden sexual excitement. She chose to ignore it—and him. He attached his leg and then stood up naked in front of her. Quickly, he walked over to the bed and lay down on it. Then he said, "Join me. I am hungry for you."

*Is our relationship ready for this intimacy?* she asked herself. She did not respond to him in any way; she stood perfectly still.

"You think that I am less of a man and that I can't perform, don't you?" he said.

"No, not at all, but I think it will take time for everything to heal," she answered, even though she had her doubt in her heart as to their future.

"'But,' nothing. Come here," he said softly, sitting on top of the bed.

She moved closer to him.

"But nothing," he said again, "but I want your butt!" Then, with a sultry look on his face, he undid the buttons on her blouse. He stared at her large breasts and then softly ran his hands over the contours of their shape. "Yum, yum," he whispered in a sexy tone. Then he reached behind her and unzipped her skirt. Immediately, her skirt fell to the floor. She leaned closer, and he softly kissed her moist lips, and that accelerated into further deep kissing.

She put her knee on the bed and catapulted her body into his arms.

He nibbled on her ear to caress and excite her. He quickly lifted her slip and pulled her panties down while still madly kissing her lips. He stroked the inside of her thighs and through her pubic hair.

She could feel his fingers within her vagina, searching and stimulating her. She stroked his hard penis. It had been a long time for both of them. Then, in one swift movement, she was on his lap, and she was going up and down vigorously.

He raised her up and down with his strong, steel-like arms until he released himself and fell into an ecstatic state that he hadn't experienced for a long time. She rolled off him and had to catch her breath, as she was in another climactic cloud herself.

They lay there in each other's arms, still feeling the physical remnants of lovemaking.

"Bet you thought that I couldn't do it anymore," Alistar said.

"I never said that," she softly replied, although he was right about what she was thinking.

"I'm running late," she said. "I better go if I am to catch the bus back to Boston."

"I'll drive up next weekend to see you," he declared.

"What?" She had been halfway out the door but turned back to look at him. She couldn't believe what she was hearing. "You are not ready for that!"

"Oh yes, I am ready for you and for driving!"

# CHAPTER SIXTEEN

## Back Again

The following Saturday, there was a knock at Ava's door, and there stood Alistar! The girls were ecstatic to finally see him again, as was Ava. After all the greetings ended, Ava went back into the kitchen to finish washing the dishes. Alistar followed her and wrapped his arms around her aproned waist and gave her a smooch on her neck. She tilted her head to the side as a way to capture his stray kiss and the warmth of it in the crevice of her neck. Then she said, "Shh! The girls might come in and see us."

"Hello, my darling," he softly whispered, ignoring her words.

"Don't you 'darling' me. I don't think you are ready for all this driving up here now."

"Oh, I am ready! It feels good to get back to my life, if you know what I mean. As a matter of fact, the insurance company is going to settle the loss of my house. I'm getting tired of being in the apartment. I was thinking that it is probably time to get a bigger house up here for all of us to live in. We would marry, of course."

"Maybe it's too soon." She gulped and swallowed with a wide-eyed expression.

"You are hesitating again," he said, reading her hidden feelings.

"I'm not the one hesitating this time. You didn't even tell your brother that you were engaged! Even worse, he was shocked when I introduced Trevor as 'our son.' He almost choked."

"You want everything in a nice little package, Ava. All tied up in a pretty bow, but life isn't like that," he said.

"Why didn't you tell him about us? Why didn't you tell him or your mother that you had a son?" Her words came out as a snarl. She drained the dishwater from the sink and slowly wiped her hands on the edge of her apron. It was a maneuver designed to wipe her sweaty hands to calm and decrease her frustration and anger.

"I'm not that close to my family anymore, and it never came up. Sometimes, I think you have no intention of marrying me. Seriously, I feel like you still cannot forgive me for abandoning you. I know things were tough on you, and I truly admire you for all your strength and resilience. You are a true survivor! Then you got pregnant again and still had the endurance to carry on, despite your hardships. After that, you had five more babies! Who does that? Then you took care of your husband when he became ill. You are just incredible! I know things could have been easier if I'd helped, but I was in military service, doing what was dictated to me for the country. Call it search and destroy the enemy! Try to survive without being killed! Make it safe for everyone else!

Silence.

"You know of the things that happened to me. The loss of Margaret and Allie brought us back together again. I know we both have irreparable pasts, and it is like some strange gravitational hold that determines our paths, but you must forgive me! The legacy of humanity is to forgive. Yes, it seems like we have numerous choices in front of us, but I am choosing you. Even Christ forgave his enemies when he was resurrected. Let me make this crystal clear: I truly love you and I want us to get married!" Immediately, he turned from her and went over to the dining room window and gazed out.

Ava started to cry, causing her vision to blur. She approached Alistar from behind and gently touched his shoulders, trying to comfort and console him. She felt his shoulder muscles stiffen as she touched him.

He said, "I know you have had a queue of men in your life, but I want to be the next. I am the one from the beginning and will be the one in the end to take care of you. I can give you a life with amenities. You know when you look at our lives way back then and now, in the present, we are different people; we have grown and matured. We can make this work. Please give me the chance!"

Ava had to think fast. A daunting feeling came over her, telling her that this was the last chance he was going to give her. She decided to forgive him. "Yes, yes, yes!" she cried, and they gently embraced.

The girls came into the room and watched them, puzzled. Ava stepped out of his embrace and said to them, "We are going to get married!"

Over the next months, they looked for a house. Alistar wanted a big colonial with at least five bedrooms.

Ava was still upset at having to sell her small bungalow. It was a gift from Devon's family to help support Mary. Ironically, Mary had sacrificed the most for the survival of the family. Her personality was affected, as she was very docile and quiet with hardly any friends or a social life. Ava came to realize that Mary took the brunt of her sin—her being pregnant with Trevor and then Mary. Now, Trevor was doing well, attending West Point, and he even had his biological father in his life to guide him. The only thing Mary had was not knowing anything about her father or how she was conceived. Ava assumed that she had conceived Mary on the luxurious trip to Italy with Devon. *I've never told Mary who her real father was and that he wanted her*, she thought. Mary probably would have had a privileged life with Devon. Ava thought back to one time when she was pregnant, and when she told Mary, she responded with, "More work for me." Ava enjoyed sex, but Mary was the caretaker for her deeds.

Ava gave deep thought to whether she should tell Mary about her father. She decided to leave the past in the past. She was embarking on another journey now and with one heck of a step up in class! The man who took her virginity was now redeeming himself and making her Trevor legitimate.

Shortly thereafter, Ava decided to sell the house and pool the money with Alistar's. She also decided she would never tell Mary the true story of her conception.

Mutually, they finally decided on a large white colonial house with large columns and a semicircular driveway in the front. It was in a fabulous neighborhood in Dedham, and there was even an estate on the street. The house had a large foyer and two living rooms. *It reminds me of Devon's mansion in Brookline where I worked as a maid*, Ava thought. Of course, this was a newer house, at barely five years old. It wasn't as large as Devon's, but there were five bedrooms. Ava and Alistar would take the master, and Trevor would have his own room. The three older girls would share the larger bedroom, and the younger two would be in the average-sized bedroom. Mary, too, would have her own bedroom. There were three bathrooms and a conservatory off the back that overlooked an inground pool. Ava couldn't believe how beautiful the house was and couldn't wait to decorate it. Alistar insisted that they marry first.

Ava felt like a princess; her dreams were coming true! She thought of the house as her palace, and she was reigning over it—and her life!

Before they married, Alistar asked if she wanted to have another baby. Ava took a deep breath; she wasn't sure how to answer. *Is he asking because he wants one or* doesn't *want one? He lost Allie. Maybe he wants another child to cement our relationship.* Ava answered with what she thought was a safe response. "Whatever the Lord wants me to do. Any type of prophylactic measure is against my Catholic religion. If it happens, then it happens."

"While we are on the subject," Alistar said, "why on earth did you have all those babies with Scott when you were financially struggling?"

She didn't want to admit that Scott required nightly sex, that he'd insisted that he couldn't sleep without a "good release." To Scott, her purpose was a nightly fuck, and he didn't care about the consequences or the result—the five girls to whom she gave birth. He meagerly provided for them on his wages as a baker. *I was probably depressed, but he was so demanding that it was just easier to open my legs for him.* She had called it "maintenance sex," but Scott had referred to her body as an "elixir." He was good to her and the children, though. He married her, even with her past. She was only seeking to be loved.

Now, here she was, marrying the first guy who took advantage of her. *How bizarre is that?* she thought. She answered Alistar's question with, "I didn't have many choices as a single unwed mother—no education, no job, and no income. I was only a mother, trying to survive in a biased society. It was difficult."

In her heart, she regretted marrying Scott just because her father demanded it of her to make her respectable. Otherwise, she might have been available to be with Devon. She regretted not waiting.

Now, she had to leave the past in the past and move on to the future—and it did look like a fabulous future with Alistar! She was euphoric that she had this chance.

# CHAPTER SEVENTEEN

# Love and Belonging

Alistar reserved St Ann's Catholic Church for their wedding in June. Ava did not have a big wedding the first time, and Alistar wanted to give her everything she never had. Ava's father would give her away, yet it was ironic that he would give her away to the man he had wanted to shoot for deflowering his daughter, decades earlier. This would be difficult for him but joyous for her to finally reunite with her first love.

Ava took Alistar over to her parents' house so they could meet. As old as her father was, he remembered how Alistar had taken advantage of his daughter. Evan gave him a stern look and said, "If I had found you, I would have used a shotgun on you for what you did to my daughter!"

"Dad, please," Ava said, "we are making amends here. Please give us your blessing."

Alistar felt remorse for what he had done and the hardships he had caused Ava and her family. He simply said, "I am truly sorry. I truly love your daughter, and we want to marry."

Evan nodded his head in agreement and gave a crusty old Irish grin.

*That's all we're going to get from him*, Ava thought, so they left.

They planned that Mary would be the maid of honor, and all the girls would have a role in the wedding. The two younger girls would carry the train of Ava's wedding dress. The other girls would be bridesmaids. Ava asked Caroline to be a bridesmaid as well.

Alistar asked Trevor to be his best man, and he gladly accepted. He asked his brother, David, to be a groomsman, and he accepted. Alistar thought that he was offering his brother an olive branch so that they would become closer again. Ava's brothers, Jerry and Tony, would also be groomsmen. Tom was included as groomsman, as he was the one who suggested that Alistar seek out Ava.

The reception was to be at the estate down the street. Alistar wanted that place because of the staircase, which he described as a huge staircase that his beautiful bride could walk down and mesmerize all who watched her with her stunning beauty. The staircase seemed to float in the air and would be a majestic backdrop for Ava to appear.

Ava decided to wear the simple single-strand pearl necklace that Devon had bought her. This way, Devon could be with her—symbolically around her neck and spiritually in her heart. Alistar requested that she wear a white gown, but Ava wasn't comfortable doing that—she had seven children, after all, and they both had been married previously. In Alistar's eyes, she was lily white, but she just couldn't bring herself to wear a white gown. Instead, she chose an off-white gown with a low-cut front and back. A lace overlay went up to her collarbone so it had a peekaboo effect on her shoulders and cleavage. The back showed her bare skin as it dipped and highlighted her curves down to her waist. The dress had a cinched waist and came out full to the floor. She had a short but simple train on the back that was an extension of the fabric layers of the dress. She knew that the dress and she would look elegant.

Ava sent a wedding invitation to her friend Emily, who came out to visit Ava a few days ahead of the wedding. She had moved to Colorado and now had three children. Ava was with Emily when they went to the social club and first met Alistar and Tom. Now, they renewed their friendship.

"How ironic that you're marrying Alistar after all these years," Emily said.

Ava told her the story of Alistar losing a leg in the war and then losing his wife and daughter in a car accident.

"You've had such hardship, Ava, including being alone with Alistar's baby. I admire how you persevered to get to this point. I wish you total happiness!"

Ava's mother came by the day before the ceremony, even though her health was deteriorating due to old age. Both parents were very forgetful, and her mother suffered from severe arthritis. Kaelyn cared for their parents, and Ava felt bad that she couldn't help much with their care, as she had to work and care for her children. The tables had turned, as she had practically raised Kaelyn many years ago. Now, it was Kaelyn who was caring for their parents. *Reap what you sow*, thought Ava. Kaelyn and her mother gave Ava their blessings.

"It's about time that you find true happiness!" Kaelyn said.

Alistar's mother was grateful that Alistar and Ava were happy and that she had a new grandson. She was becoming very fond of Ava.

Tom, Alistair's navy buddy, arrived for the wedding with his wife. Alistar was truly happy to see him. Who would have known that they would all be together to witness the long-separated happy couple getting married? Everyone was overjoyed!

On their wedding day, Alistar waited patiently at the altar in his black tuxedo.

A white horse and buggy brought Ava and her entourage to the church. They lined up at the back of the church to walk down the aisle. When the first notes of the wedding march played, Ava became anxious but knew she had to wear a smile. She turned to her girls, who were standing behind her, and apprehensive as they displayed goofy nervous smirks and giggles. Her way of calming them down was to distract them by saying something silly, "listen, we must all wear our smiles, so get them out of your back pockets and put them on."

Mary and Caroline went down the aisle first, then the three older girls. Ava was next, on her father's arm. They smiled as they looked out at all the people in the pews. Directly behind Ava were her two younger girls, holding her train.

The groomsmen were lined up at the altar with Alistar.

The wedding march stopped, and Ava took her place beside Alistar. He looked incredibly handsome! The fragrance of the flowers enhanced their joyous union. Ava glanced at Alistar with a nervous smile. He returned a warm smile. They turned together to face the priest.

During the ceremony, Ava gently stroked the pearl necklace that delicately hung at her neck. She felt like the necklace clung to her soul, and she rubbed it gently; it was her only true connection to Devon.

The priest spoke of a weeping willow tree, which represented Ava and Alistar, as it swayed from side to side; it would always grow and be in motion. Then he referred to their union as a second-bloom unification. Ava silently laughed at that metaphor.

The priest said, "In the pageantry of life, we display numerous facades, but with integrity and righteousness as our guides, true happiness will be our legacy."

They placed the rings on each other's fingers and both said "I do".

Then the priest said to Alistar, "You may kiss your bride."

Alistar lifted her veil and gave her a long and passionate kiss.

The crowd applauded vigorously! Both Ava and Alistar were ecstatic and waved as they walked back down the aisle, followed by the groomsmen and bridesmaids.

Outside, they were congratulated and hugged! Copious amounts of rice were tossed in the air and landed on them.

The horse and buggy awaited them. Alistar assisted Ava, in her long, flowing gown, into the buggy. Everyone waved with happy smiles as the driver guided the buggy on its course.

Shortly afterward, they reached the estate and walked across the lush, manicured grounds. The photographer had them pose outside and took many pictures. Finally, they went into the estate. Alistar and Ava were introduced, and they walked arm in arm down the grand freestanding staircase. Alistar stopped four steps from the bottom and said, "We are both so happy to finally be united in holy matrimony!" He gave Ava another passionate kiss, leaning her back over his arm—he had practiced this many times so he could keep his artificial leg in place. Everyone gave a big cheer!

Large banquet tables were set up in a massive drawing room, and everyone took their seats. Crepe-paper wedding decorations hung from all sides of the room and enhanced the wedding festivities.

Trevor asked everyone to stand as the wedding couple sat down. He gave a toast. "I have finally found my biological father, and to find that he and my mother are still in love is a true miracle. Best wishes to them and this union!" He raised his champagne glass and toasted the happy couple. Everyone else in the room did the same. Then they all applauded the couple.

Alistar gave Ava another kiss, and then all the guests started tapping the sides of their glasses as a gesture for them to kiss more. Finally, Alistar said, "Please stop! We will never get to the meal otherwise—although I love kissing my lovely bride!"

Everyone laughed, and then the waitresses came out, serving the lavish four-course meal. After everyone finished, Alistar and Ava cut the wedding cake and served a mouthful to each other. The guests applauded them again.

Next was the first dance together as husband and wife. The three-piece band played her favorite song, "Stardust," and Ava felt like a queen. She and Alistar made eyes at each other, and then Alistar whispered in her ear, "Second-bloom relationship or not, you will always be my first bloom! I love you!"

Ava giggled and then replied, "Well, they say why buy the cow when you get the milk for free, but this time there are no returns!"

Last of all, the couple went around the room together and thanked their guests for coming.

When they got to Tom's table, Ava thanked him and then turned to his wife, Cherie, and extended her hand to thank her for coming to their wedding.

"So crazy that we should be here at your wedding," Tom said. He stood up to take her hand and leaned over to give her a kiss on her cheek.

"Yes, and it is good to see you! Thank you for being a part of Alistar's life and participating in our wedding," Ava said with a broad smile.

"You look beautiful, absolutely stunning!" Tom said.

Ava blushed. "Thank you."

"Who would have known that after all these years, you two would be a couple? Back in those days, we had Prohibition, and we couldn't drink. How awful that was! Of course, we sailors were resourceful and found alcohol. Now, the alcoholic spirits are limitless! How things have changed!" exclaimed Tom.

"Too funny," replied Alistar.

"I heard it was because of you reminding Alistar about me that he decided to look me up," Ava said.

"Yes, as a matter of fact, I *did* encourage him to look you up," Tom said.

"Thank you for that," Ava said sincerely. "Otherwise, we never would have found each other again."

"Guess my friend Alistar, here, missed the boat, so to speak, way back when the USS *Donovan* sailed out of port!" Tom teased.

Ava giggled. "Yes, and my heart with it!"

"You found each other again—that's all that matters!" Tom said.

Later, Ava sat down at Emily's table and they talked about old times and about growing up together. Then Ava and Alistar took Emily to Tom's table.

"Emily, you remember Tom, and this is his wife, Cherie," Ava said. It was a quirky type of reunion, as Emily had dated Tom, but everyone got along.

Alistar chuckled. "I am truly happy that I finally have my son and Ava!"

Then the couple stopped at Caroline's table, where she sat with her husband and three children. Ava and Caroline hugged each other and Ava thanked her for being part of the wedding party. Then Caroline introduced Ava and Alistar to her husband, Michael, and their children.

"We should get together after you return from your honeymoon," Michael said.

Ava was intrigued with meeting Michael, whom Caroline had said was in the Mafia. A slight chill went up her spine as she remembered that.

The evening ended, and Alistar and Ava dressed in their going-away clothes. They returned down the grand staircase, and the crowd circled around them. They sincerely thanked everyone again for coming to their wedding.

"We now have new horizons to reach so we can make more memories!" Alistar announced.

Ava whispered in his ear, "Memories that fill me with tears of joy, just being with you!"

They left the estate in Alistar's waiting car, which had a JUST MARRIED sign on the back. It was covered with different colored streamers from the engine hood to the trunk of the vehicle in a festive manner. There were old boots tied to the bumper that thumped as they drove. Ava turned one last time to bid a last goodbye to the crowd as she embarked on her journey with Alistar. She had no regrets. *Everything will be fine now*, she thought. She felt delirious, enthusiastic, and overflowed with happiness!

They drove to Niagara Falls for their honeymoon. They both felt they were beginning a wonderful life together. The hotel had a view of Bridal Veil Falls, which

Ava thought was romantic and appropriate for their situation. "Did you plan it this way?" she asked Alistar, but he only chuckled in response.

They could hear the millions of gallons of water flowing over the falls into the lower water basins. The atmosphere had a murky moisture in thick, cloud patterns that would consume a person's entire body. The fog appeared as smoke due to thick, misty droplets.

Ava gazed at her husband as they stepped out onto the balcony. They could see the reflection of the moonlight as it danced within the ripples from the force of the flowing water. They kissed on the balcony and melted away the tiny droplets of mist between them.

Soon, he guided her to the large bed, and they spent the rest of the twilight hours in lovemaking. "You are my hidden cache of treasure," Alistar told her.

"We are two soul mates who fate divided but destiny reunited," Ava answered.

The next day, they went sightseeing. They took a boat ride on the Lower Falls, which had breathtaking views of all the falls. There were clear pockets where they could get a glimpse of the coastal mountainous landscape from the depths of the magnificent gorge. The topography seemed to suddenly change after they came out of the steamy mist of the inner falls. The gravitational pull on the magnificent flowing water made bubbling, rippling lace-like patterns. Later, they walked the romantic pathways around the falls. They found an intimate restaurant with a view of the flowing water. After dinner, they returned to their hotel room and listened to the noisy falls outside their window. They went out on the balcony to view the scenery. The heavy mist, added to the alcohol that they had consumed, made them feel almost dizzy. This led them down the pathway for sex again!

The following day, they crossed the border to the Canadian side of the falls to see the view there—more breathtaking views and photos to take!

Ava wanted a short honeymoon, as she didn't want to be away from the children too long. They both felt satisfied, happy, and ready to return home.

# CHAPTER EIGHTEEN

# Self-Actualization

When they returned from their honeymoon, they closed on the house and moved in. There was a lot to pack and new purchases to be made—living room furniture, bedroom sets, and dining room furniture. Although Ava and her family had moved frequently, this time was different, as they were moving to a grand, large house. It was fun decorating the house. Ava felt like she had finally found herself!

Life settled into a wonderfully slow pace, with the girls going to school, and Trevor graduating from West Point. Ava continued to work, but soon, Alistar convinced her to quit her job.

"We don't need the money from your job," he said. "You can stay home to raise the kids. Besides, it's costing us more in taxes for you to work because your income puts us in a higher tax bracket." He was a thrifty accountant and lived by the tax laws and deductions. He found another job as an accountant in the area.

Shortly thereafter, Ava quit her job. Mary continued her employment and took the bus to work. It took longer to get to her job from the new place, but she had her own bedroom in the new house; she also continued to care for her sisters.

One night, Alistar called out frantically in his sleep and was drenched in sweat. When he awoke the following morning, Ava asked him about it.

"It's a side effect of being in the war. They call it shell-shock," he said. "The episodes are infrequent now, but they do continue to occur."

Alistar convinced Ava to get her driver's license. At first, she showed trepidation, but he took her out for a few lessons, and finally, she got the hang of it. She felt like a pioneer, as few other women were driving. When she finally had a little experience behind her, he purchased a convertible Ford Carson for her. It was an impressive, large-bodied, eye-catching automobile. On the fenders were curved large mountains that elongated to peaks. The hood inclined upward to match the fenders but sat higher. The silhouette resembled a majestic mountain range. A grill in the front of the vehicle made the two circular headlights look like two smiling eyes. The white roof contrasted with the car's deep-blue exterior, making it stand out. There was a sideboard for her to step on to get into the vehicle. The fenders tapered down to shiny silvered sculptured rims that housed whitewall tires. She drove the car only locally, but she looked stunning in the highly polished dark-blue machine with its dark-blue leather interior.

One day, she was driving down a hill and hit a fire hydrant. A flume of water came gushing out, causing her to lose control of the vehicle. Then she hit the fence behind the hydrant. It was located near the local elementary school, and the children were being dismissed. She caused quite a bit of commotion! Ava was so embarrassed, as people had seen the accident and came running over to her. She was fine but stunned.

Alistar was soon on the scene. He was only concerned that she was OK, as he had a brief moment when it reminded him of the accident when Margaret and Allie were killed. Immediately, he controlled the memory. He was thankful that Ava did not have any life-threatening injuries.

About a month later, the doorbell rang. Ava answered the door to find Brendon, Devon's son. She was surprised to see him and asked him to come in. He now had a remarkable resemblance to Devon—same height, facial features, and hair color. In Ava's heart, it seemed as if Devon was standing in front of her.

Ava invited him to sit down in the living room and then offered him a refreshment, which he declined. She sat down on the sofa across from him.

"You look well," he said.

"Thank you. I assume that you are well too?"

"Yes, but let me get straight to the point: I'm here to

discuss the use of the money that you inherited from the estate."

Ava narrowed her eyes. "Yes?"

"I hear that you married and obviously bought this nice home," he said, sizing up the room.

"Yes, I did marry."

"Well, as you know, the money was for Mary's care and was to be used for her. I assume that it was not joined with your new husband's affairs. You did sell the house on Poplar Street?"

"Yes, I sold the house on Poplar Street."

"I want to make sure that the assets from my father go to her."

Ava knew that she had to think fast. She hadn't liked selling her house and using the proceeds for this house. Unfortunately, she'd had no choice; they wouldn't have had enough money to purchase this house otherwise. "I still weep for your father and have high admiration for him. He was like no other—so brilliant and ebullient," she said fondly.

"Thank you. I miss him too," Brendon answered as he slightly bowed his head. "I hope that you separated the proceeds, and it is safe for Mary's use."

"I can tell that you miss your father terribly. I know that money was for Mary's care, and I have fulfilled that stipulation. In fact, she lives here, and the money is still used for her benefit."

"There was enough money there for Mary to have an income, if it was used properly."

Ava bristled at his words. "She's fine, and you

needn't worry. We are all happy here. Maybe you should leave now."

Silence penetrated the thick air between them. Brendon's jaw was set in a firm grimace that matched the cold stare on his face. He got up and walked to the front door and out of the house. Just as he was getting into his car, Mary was approaching the house on the sidewalk. She looked at Brendon but had no idea who he was.

When Mary went into the house, her mother was still on the couch in a contemplative pose. "Who was that who just left?" she asked.

"Oh, no one … just a salesman," answered Ava. Brendon had made her feel guilty about her use of Mary's money. Now it would weigh on her conscience.

Mary thought there was something odd about the "salesman." She had noticed that he almost had the same type of wiry dark-auburn hair as she did. He was about the same age too. She dismissed the coincidence and started supper for the girls.

A week later, Mary returned from work one evening to find a letter waiting for her on the mail table near the front door. She took the letter up to her room. There was no return address on it. She opened the letter and read, "I am your half-brother, Brendon, and I want to meet you. …"

She ran out of her room and screamed for her mother!

Ava came running from the kitchen and saw Mary screaming at the top of the stairs. She was yelling, "Brendon! Brendon! Brendon!"

Ava knew her deep dark secret about Mary's father was about to be exposed. Ava ran to the top of the stairs. She put her arm around Mary, but Mary shrugged it off.

Mary screeched at the top of her voice, "Is this Brendon who he says he is?"

"Quiet down," Ava said as she guided Mary into her room. They sat on the bed, and Ava said, "Many years ago, I had sex with a man named Devon, and I became pregnant with you. He was estranged from his wife, with whom he had a son named Brendon. I don't regret having you. I love you dearly!"

"So you not only had relations with Trevor's father but also with a married guy named Devon!" Mary's face showed her disgust.

Ava's heart pounded in her chest. This was something that she never wanted to address, especially not with her daughter who was the result of that intercourse.

"So you lifted your dress and let these men get into your panties," Mary went on. "What are you? A floozy? No wonder you never told me about my father! Now I have a half-brother? I know he was the young man who left the house last week—the one you said was a 'salesman'! Liar! Get out of my room!" She pointed her index finger toward the door.

Ava left the room, as Mary demanded.

Mary did not talk to Ava for an entire week. Ava attempted to make conversation, but Mary ignored her. Then, after supper one night, Mary announced, "I'm going to meet Brendon tomorrow night."

211

Ava asked, "Do you think that is wise?" She had been a nervous wreck about this situation, and now Mary was going to meet Brendon. *I know damn well that I'll be the topic of conversation!* She wondered if her enemy, Jane would be a part of this, trying to discredit her.

"I will meet him and find out everything!"

The next evening, Brendon came for Mary in his sports car. Ava watched out the living room window as they left.

The following morning, Mary slept late, as Ava tried to control her constantly erupting anxiety. Finally, Mary got up and took a shower. Then she went downstairs and sat alone at the breakfast table.

Ava approached her and asked, "How did everything go last evening?"

"I learned a lot. I heard how my father was still married, and you had an affair, how you tried to commit suicide by sticking your head in a gas oven when you were pregnant with me, how they wanted to take me and raise me, and how you received an *inheritance* for my care! I guess that says it all!" She abruptly stood up. "I will be moving out next weekend."

Ava cried, as all her sins were exposed with terrible consequences! She only had been looking for love but constant complications intertwined in her life from the very beginning!

The following weekend, as Mary moved out, Alistar put his arm around Ava and said, "Let her go. She will have to find her own way."

# CHAPTER NINETEEN

# The Past Resurfaces

Ava started socializing and became active at the school that the girls attended. Now they were spread between middle school and high school. She enjoyed not being fearful of where her next meal would come from and the stability of their lives. The memory of having to move to avoid paying rent was starting to fade too. *How my life has changed!*

She helped out with bake sales to benefit the school, which used the extra money for sports activities and extra supplies. Ava chaperoned school dances to make sure the children were safe and having clean fun. She met other mothers and enjoyed life while raising the rest of her daughters. Caroline and she became great friends and did a lot of benefit activities together.

It seemed funny to Ava that Caroline never mentioned anything personal to her, other than that her husband was in the Mafia. Ava couldn't imagine what that must be like.

Sometimes, Ava would compare her past plight of

poverty to Caroline's situation. Caroline came from a wealthy family in Italy, but she had an arranged marriage to an American. No one had told her that he was in the Mafia. *Caroline's situation was more than likely worse than mine was*, Ava thought. Sometimes, Caroline would ask Ava about Devon, and Ava would relate her memories of him almost as if he was still alive. They had a wonderful friendship, and Ava never asked Caroline about her personal business; she respected her friend's privacy.

Jenna, Ava's second daughter, started dating a neighborhood boy. Ava didn't want any of her girls to be taken advantage of, as she had been. She especially did not want any of her daughters to suffer the effects and repercussions of an unplanned pregnancy. Even though she loved her children immensely, her life was controlled by her one mistake of having premarital sex. How ironic that decades later—through hardships, forgiveness, and love—she would end up married to Alistar, her first encounter. *Bizarre that something that once doomed me has now repositioned me*, she thought. Still, Ava knew only too well what can happen to young, immature girls.

Ava sat down with Jenna and explained sexual intercourse. She emphasized the significance of not getting pregnant before marriage. Ava wanted to use herself as an example, but she couldn't bring herself to talk about her own mistakes with her daughter. Of course, the family now knew that Alistar was Trevor's biological father, and they seemed to accept that, but she wanted to keep hidden the secret of how Mary was conceived. Now that Mary had moved out, Ava hoped that her secret would be safe, but she was always fearful that Mary would return and disclose it. Ava didn't want to admit that she was stupid enough to make the same mistake twice.

She tried to explain to Jenna about responsibility and consequences. She hoped she had impressed upon her daughter to play it safe and not let her guard down. She preached abstinence over and over. In addition, Ava decided to supply as much supervision as possible—one of the reasons she was a chaperone at the dances.

Ava didn't know, however, that Jenna was sneaking out at night. Her boyfriend had a car, and one night, when they parked in front of the house, Ava looked out and saw them kissing in the car. Ava was frantic as she ran outside.

"Get out of the car and go in the house!" she screamed at Jenna.

After that, Ava drove around at night to the areas where the young ones would hang out and "neck." One night, she saw Jenna's boyfriend's car. The windows were fogged up and steamy, and she knew that meant a lot of heavy breathing was going on. She pulled her car up behind them and shone her high beams into the back window of their car. Then she frantically honked her horn a few times. She then walked up to the passenger side and saw Jenna sitting there with her clothes in disarray. Ava pounded on the window, yelling, "Get out of there and get into my car!" Then Ava proceeded to scream at the boy.

Meanwhile, the other parked cars started up their

engines and formed a line, as if they were in a parade to exit the parking area.

When Ava and Jenna arrived home, there was more yelling and screaming at each other. Alistar intervened at one point, saying, "Jenna, your mother is only being cautious so that nothing happens to you."

"Like what you two did when you made Trevor?" Jenna shouted. "Who are you to talk, when you did the very same thing?"

"Youthful thoughts and behavior in immature minds only lead to disaster," Alistar told her. "Sexual attraction in youth, compounded with raging impulses, can only doom you. You must be ready to truly love another person—trust me, I know!"

Jenna glared at him disrespectfully and yelled, "Shut up!"

Alistar was speechless. Quickly, he turned to leave the room and muttered under his breath, "This generation's decadence is certainly deteriorating to a new low."

Things continued to be difficult between them, and Ava eventually grounded her for a month.

Jenna was in her last year of high school when, one day, she came crying to Ava that she had made a mistake.

Ava knew exactly what Jenna meant.

Ava and Alistar joined with the boy's family and gave Jenna and her boyfriend a small wedding. They then got an apartment. Ava's heart was broken, and she prayed that it would not be as hard for Jenna to survive as she herself had experienced. *Jenna's better off, though*, Ava thought. *Her boyfriend did marry her. She won't suffer the judgmental comments or being called a slut like I was.*

Jenna had a baby boy, and they named him Joseph. Ava was delighted with the baby and helped to care for him. Finally, she was able to enjoy a baby without hardships.

Ava and Caroline joined a gardening group in the neighborhood. One neighbor had a greenhouse, and the ladies would plant items there. They would take turns watering and caring for the young seedlings. In the spring, when most of the plants bloomed, they would have a get-together and show off their work. They entered into small contests around the area, and the sale of the plants benefitted charities. Ava found this enjoyable; she liked the companionship, the planting, and the general fun of the events.

For one event, the club president rented a hotel hall for a benefit, with the proceeds going to sick children. All the members enjoyed putting the event together. Everyone had a role or two.

There were many patrons attending the well-publicized benefit. Ava and Caroline shared a table. Ava had her back turned, fixing some plants and tying ribbons around the containers, when someone called her name.

Ava turned and saw Jane standing there with dagger like eyes unequivocally cemented on her! Ava's stomach dropped and felt like it was going to fall out of her body. *Oh no!* thought Ava.

"Well, look what we have here!" Jane sneered. "Looks like you are citizen of the year. I hear that you remarried and have a nice house and a nice lifestyle now."

Ava stood silent; it was as if a meteor storm had hit the hall. *Brendon must have told her*, she thought. *Did he put her up to this? Is he still upset with how I handled Mary's money?*

She knew that Mary had spent time with Brendon; she didn't even know where Mary was since she had moved out.

"You go around and play a game like you are a wonderful person," Jane said. "Do they know about your past? You stole my husband and got knocked up by him. Then you had two illegitimate babies! What a woman you are, you slut!"

Everyone was looking in their direction as Jane continued to cause a scene. All the conversation and movement in the room seemed to freeze as people focused on the scene between the two.

In a controlled tone, Ava said, "Look, I didn't steal your husband."

"You did! You did! You are nothing but a slut—a whore!" Jane ranted, waving her arms in the air for added drama.

"At least *I* am not a slut who deceived my husband about being the father of my baby!" Ava shot back. "Especially a man I was still married to! I took life and dealt with whatever fate gave me. You deceived Devon by pretending to be pregnant with his baby when the whole time you were knocked up by another guy! No one does that! You are the loose one here! You only have yourself to blame! I am sorry for your misfortune, but we all make our own beds, don't we?" She firmly crossed her arms in front of her body, as if to stand guard against Jane's waving arms.

Jane pointed her finger in Ava's face. "Cunt!" she spat at her.

Someone obviously had called the police, as they suddenly were there, where Jane and Ava were still involved in the intense confrontation.

The police instructed Jane to leave. She lowered her head, turned, and abruptly left the hall.

All eyes were on Ava. Her deepest secrets had been exposed. She walked over to the president of the garden club and said, "I have to leave. I don't feel well." In truth, she was humiliated! She waved goodbye to Caroline, who was still at the table, stunned.

Ava cried all the way home. She could feel her sins resurfacing and reopening now; the pain of her youth again haunted her. She knew that she had made mistakes, but she felt that she had paid for her sins. "All I ever wanted was to be loved!" she cried. Stupidly, she had made love when she should have waited until she was married. She truly loved her children and that was the stimulus for her to carry on. She had survived when all odds were against her.

When she arrived home, Alistar was reading the newspaper in the living room chair. He arose when he saw her come in. "What's wrong?" he asked when he saw the look on her face, and he quickly wrapped his arms around her.

"Jane—Devon's wife—turned up at the benefit, and we had a confrontation! She called me a slut and said that I had two illegitimate babies. Our reputation is ruined! The police were called!" Ava sobbed against Alistar's chest.

"Oh darling, I am so sad to hear that. She means nothing!" He spoke calmly to console her and rubbed her back with soothing strokes. Her wet tears soaked his shirt as she cried. "Why don't we go out for dinner?" he asked, hoping to distract her.

"No," she sobbed, with heaving breaths.

"She is just another jerk along the journey in life that we encounter. Remember that you have to clear the weeds to let the flowers grow. Don't let her get to you. What about a ride?" he asked.

She didn't answer.

"Go upstairs and freshen up. We will go out for an ice cream and a nice drive."

She nodded her head in agreement and retreated upstairs. When she came back downstairs, they went for a ride in her convertible. Alistar drove to Milton and around the streets that led to the Blue Hills. Alistar parked his car at the base of the hill, and they took a walk up the hill through the forest trails.

They talked about the encounter with Jane.

"She's nothing," Alistar said, "other than a big, bad bag of wind. "Think of her as the Big Bad Wolf, but in the end, the good Goldilocks survives."

Ava took his hand and smiled at such a silly scenario.

"You're mixing up your fairy tales," she said, "but she will blow my house down!"

"She will certainly try, but everything you need to know is in the truth of a fairy tale."

They took each other's hands and continued up the hill.


That year, Pearl Harbor was bombed, and the battle of Normandy ensued. Americans were outraged by what the Japanese had done on American shores. The military responded.

Trevor had been working in a secret role for the military in Washington, DC. Ava was worried that he probably would be sent overseas. He received his orders and was to be sent to France the following week. He had one week at home before he was to be deployed.

Ava had a difficult time keeping her anxiety in check and masking her worries. Alistar did not show any emotion. He knew that Trevor would have to do whatever the military asked of him to defend the country.

Trevor had met a girl at a college dance when he was at West Point. Her name was Natasha, and they were crazy about each other. She was from a good family in Cambridge, Massachusetts. He spent most of his time with her before leaving, but they all went to a restaurant the evening before he was to leave and had a going away party for him. It was a difficult day for everyone.

The next day, when he left, Ava couldn't stop crying. Every day thereafter, she prayed for him on the pearl necklace that Devon had given to her as if it was a set of rosary beads. She did this to console her heart.

# EPILOGUE

One day, Ava came home to find that Alistar was excited. The *Boston News* wanted to do an article on him about his naval career during The Great War. They wanted to compare his experiences with those of the servicemen who were now embarking on another World War. He wrote an essay on the events—that he had been in the navy for twenty years, that his ship exploded after hitting an underwater mine, and that many men gave their lives unselfishly for this country. He wrote that freedom is not free. He described his time when they dismantled other countries' military bases. Never once did he mention his sacrifices; he didn't write about being in a coma for a year, losing a leg, or the psychological trauma that still surfaced from time to time.

Alistar was very proud of his service to the country, and when the article was published, everyone saw his contributions. When anyone called him a true hero, though, he would reply, "We did what was needed and never asked questions. It was a true honor to serve America and defend democracy."

Ava was so proud of him. She had achieved everything

that she ever wanted. Of course, not knowing Mary's whereabouts caused a constant emptiness in her heart, but she remained hopeful that someday they would reconcile.

Alistar and Ava would sit together on a glider swing on the front porch, holding hands and gliding back and forth in a synchronized motion for hours at a time after supper. They had a solid, structured lifestyle with all the pleasures of the times.

One day, Alistar said to Ava, "We are truly happy! I know our lives together have been a combination of the aftereffects of our experiences, but that brought wisdom."

"I would describe our life together as more of a combination of aftershocks from a severe earthquake, which brought wisdom! Yes, dear, when the right thing is done, then happiness and satisfaction are sure to follow."

"In the pageantry of life, we display numerous facades, but with integrity and righteousness as our guides, true happiness will be our legacy!" Alistar said, and he planted a kiss on her cheek.

Later that evening, they took a relaxing stroll around the pond. Alistar rolled up his pant legs and removed his shoes to dip his feet in the water. He left two footprints in the sand—one from his own foot and the other from his prosthesis. The imprints were practically identical on the sandy shoreline.

A special thank you to Alfred Riley, iUniverse Publishing, who provided guidance and support.

Also by Janet Perroni

*Ava*
(Eric Hoffer First Prize Romance 2021)
(Eric Hoffer First Prize Horizon Award 2021)

https://www.jperroniauthor.com